Motor Mouth

The kid wouldn't shut up. He fired questions at Grady all the way to Fourth Street like he thought Grady was the Welcome Wagon lady or something.

"You're Grady, right? My mom told me we're going to be living in the same house. I've never lived next door to a friend before."

Grady shot the kid a glare. Friend? What was he talking about?

"We're from Walding," said Burgess. "Ever heard of it?"

Grady shook his head. Maybe Walding wasn't a town. Maybe it was a planet. Way out there, past Pluto someplace.

Other Bullseye Books you will enjoy

GRADY
the GREAT

----

by
Judith Bernie Strommen

Judith Bernie Strommen

BULLSEYE BOOKS • ALFRED A. KNOPF
NEW YORK

For Marion Dane Bauer,
who gave me wizard shoes,
And for the Tuesday Night Writers,
who helped me lace them up

And for Kizzy

Library of Congress Catalog Card Number: 90-4694
ISBN: 0-679-83469-9
RL: 4.9
First Bullseye Books edition: April 1993

Manufactured in the United States of America
10 9 8 7 6 5 4 3 2 1

New York, Toronto, London, Sydney, Auckland

Contents

1

Dear Mouse

Grady Hunstiger did not believe in writing letters. Ordinarily. As he told his grandmother who lived in Cincinnati and wanted something besides bills in her mailbox, writing letters was hazardous to his health. It made him anxious and jumpy. The telephone worked much better; he didn't have to spell every word he said.

But when he took a good look at how things were going, that first week of summer vacation, it was clear they were anything but ordinary.

Like it wasn't every day that a guy's best friend deserted him. A friend who'd shared baseball cards, Popsicles, paper routes, and the chicken pox with him, and lived under the same roof besides.

Grady sat on the edge of his bed and ran his fingers

over the patch of plaster that the landlord had spread on the wall. It set him to thinking.

He and Mouse had been the luckiest kids in Johnson Falls, Minnesota, living only a wall apart in the old Cooney house. When it had been turned into a home for two families, Grady's mom had rented the right half. A few days later Mouse's family, the Stotts, had moved into the other side. That was almost seven years ago, which, to a guy who's eleven, is a pretty big chunk of his life.

They'd been the luckiest kids, all right. A real team. Grady the Great and the Mighty Mouse. But all that was over now, because two weeks ago Mouse and his parents had climbed into their car and driven off into the sunset. They'd waved and hollered, Mr. Stott blinking his taillights all the way down the street.

The problem was, they weren't going on vacation. They were moving. And not to the next town or to the next state, but halfway across the country. Culver City, California.

Two time zones away.

Grady pushed his thumb up against the plaster to see if it would leave a mark. It did. The plaster was still damp.

It wasn't that there weren't other kids around, because there were. It wasn't that he didn't have other friends, because he did. It's just that they weren't Mouse. And without Mouse, things weren't right at all.

There was only one solution. It would require extraordinary effort, but then these were extraordinary circumstances. A guy did what he had to do.

So Grady went to his desk and pulled a piece of paper out of the drawer. He found a pencil stub and sat down to write a letter.

Dear Mouse,

 Are you there yet?

 Mom said it takes time to drive 1,743 miles. But you've been at it for almost a week now. I figure you should be all moved in.

 I hope you get to use the autograph book I gave you. It cost me $3.25, but I was glad to do it.

 Things aren't looking too good here. Without you on the pitcher's mound, we're 0–3. Plus my bike is broken again. Wendy-Alice (Bossyface herself) got braces. She is even uglier now, if you can believe that.

 Your side of the house is still empty. Mr. Peavey fixed the peephole in the bedroom wall. Who told on us?

 The big reason I am writing you is this. I might buy a bus ticket and visit you. Would that be okay?

      Your best friend,
      Grady Hunstiger
P.S. Bossyface wants your address. Write me back soon or I might have to give it to her.

Grady drew a picture of a Greyhound bus at the bottom of the letter. He wrote the words CALIFORNIA EXPRESS across its side. Then he drew himself waving out of the last bus window and Tiny, his gold retriever, running along behind. But it didn't look right. So he erased Tiny running behind and drew him inside the bus with his head hanging out of the second-to-last window. Perfect. Tiny would love California for sure.

When he and Tiny pulled into the bus station at Culver City, Mouse would be there, of course. His dad and mom, too. They'd be cheering and tossing confetti into the air. A marching band would begin to play the minute he and Tiny stepped off the bus. "Grady!" Mouse would beg. "Please say you'll stay *forever!*"

Grady leaned back against his desk chair and smiled. *Forever?* Well, *he'd* just figured on the summer. But leave it to Mouse to come up with the best ideas!

Why not stay forever? Why not *move* to California? His mother could find a job (one that didn't make her so tired), and they could rent a big double house with palm trees in the front yard and move in next door to the Stotts. What a brainstorm!

For the first time in a week, Grady had the feeling that things were going to work out. All he had to do now was explain the brainstorm to his mother. She would love California for sure.

He closed his eyes and was imagining his mother relaxing on the porch of a big white house in California when he heard a *slam-crunch* from outside. A metal-on-metal slam-crunch.

The daydream vanished and Grady opened his eyes. He tipped his chair toward the window and looked down at the street. A rusty blue station wagon with a U-Haul trailer hitched behind had run up over the curb in front of the house. It had smashed into the fire hydrant, which was tilting, and water was spurting into the street. People with hair the color of pumpkins were climbing out of the car, hollering.

"How could you do this!"

"I didn't see it!"

"What d'ya mean, you didn't see it?"

"Now, dear, calm down."

A skinny kid with glasses and a huge green T-shirt on was standing by the side of the car yelling, "My fish! My fish!"

Then Grady saw Tiny bound across the yard. He pressed his forehead against the screen of the open window and called out "Tiny! *No!*"

But it was too late. Grady watched Tiny pounce on a little girl as she carried a doll up the sidewalk. The doll somersaulted through the air.

Grady knocked over his desk chair as he bolted out of his room and down the stairs. He flung open the screen door and ran toward what was, by the time he got there, a tangled pile of golden fur, orange hair, legs, arms, and swooshing tail. Tiny was sitting on her, his chest puffed, his ears perked. All ninety pounds of him.

"Off, Tiny! Off!"

Grady stepped over the doll. He slipped his fingers under Tiny's collar and pulled. Reluctantly, Tiny got up. Grady was almost afraid to look. The girl was probably a pancake by now. Wile E. Coyote after the steamroller.

"Are you okay?" he asked.

The girl sat up and blinked at him. Her eyes were big like saucers.

Grady helped her up. Dirt was stuck to her cheek. Her knee was scraped. And boy, was she short. Hardly taller than a yardstick. Tiny couldn't be responsible for that, could he?

"Sorry—" Grady started to say, but the girl wasn't listening.

"Mama!" she screamed. "Bad dog!"

"Hey, wait a minute," said Grady.

She didn't. She ran toward the station wagon wailing. "Bad dog! Baaad dog!"

Grady stood with his fingers looped around Tiny's

collar and watched her go, her hair like a flying orange nest. Geez. Not only was she a shrimp, but she made things up besides. Tiny was *not* a bad dog. He was just extra friendly. Especially to people who showed up in his yard.

When the girl's parents came over to give him a lecture, he'd tell them that. After all, this was Tiny's front yard, not theirs. Who did they think they were anyway, crashing onto somebody else's property? That was trespassing, wasn't it? Maybe he ought to tell them that, too.

But no one came over to talk to him. As he waited, with Tiny leaning against him, he saw why. No one was paying attention to the little girl. They were too busy yelling at each other.

So just who *were* these people? And how could anybody (it had to be the teenager) be dumb enough to drive into a fire hydrant? Grady looked at the U-Haul trailer, and it gave him a horrible idea. No, he wouldn't think that. These people couldn't be his new neighbors. They just couldn't.

Well, he wasn't going to stand around any longer. He'd go back into the house and call the fire department about the hydrant. Then he'd get Mouse's letter ready for the mail. Before he knew it, the people would be gone.

"Come on, fella," he whispered to Tiny. "We're leaving." He scooped up the girl's raggy doll and tossed it toward the station wagon . . . so the people wouldn't forget it and have to come back.

"Hey, you! You with the dog!" The skinny kid with the T-shirt was looking at him.

"Me?" Grady pointed to himself.

"Yeah. Help me!"

Grady sighed. He squatted down in front of Tiny. "Can you behave yourself for one minute?"

Tiny lifted one front paw and wagged his tail, which meant he'd give it a try. Grady decided to take his chances. He released his hold on the collar, his fingers aching from the tight grip.

"Stay, Tiny. Please."

The kid looked terribly upset. He pointed to the car and said, "My fish!" which was no surprise to Grady, who was getting tired of hearing it.

"What fish?"

"My goldfish," the boy answered. "When Dewey hit the hydrant, the cookie jar tipped over and my goldfish fell out."

Grady didn't want to know what goldfish were doing in a cookie jar, so he didn't ask. He peered through the rolled-up windows of the station wagon. Plants, books, shoes, spilled out of boxes. A Monopoly game had overturned, and the whole backseat was covered with pink, yellow, and blue money.

"So will you help me?" The kid was close to begging.

"Okay," Grady answered, not feeling the least bit okay. But maybe if he helped, they'd be gone quicker.

The kid adjusted his glasses. "Here's the plan. I'll open the car door nice and slow. You squeeze into the backseat and get the fish. I'll hold the door closed so the cats won't escape."

"Cats?"

"Yeah, two. I swell up if I touch them. That's why I didn't get the fish myself. The cats were in boxes, but I don't know now. We were really sailing when we hit the hydrant."

The kid inched the door open. Grady took a deep breath and, pushing aside a pile of Monopoly money, slid into the backseat next to a popcorn popper. The vinyl cushion was cracked and sticky under his hand. The air smelled old.

"Where do you think they are?" he asked the boy through the open slit of door.

"The cats or the fish?"

"The fish!"

"Check the baseball gloves. Look in the frying pan."

Grady checked and looked and checked some more, until he found one fish lying on the floor under a "Get Out of Jail Free" card. Its black eye stared up at him. It was either dead or in shock.

"Here's one!" he called to the kid. He lifted it up by

its flimsy tail fin, then rolled down the window just enough to slide his hand through. He dropped the fish into the boy's waiting hand.

It was getting hot in the car, and Grady was sure he'd used up most of the air. Something was moving around under the front seat, and the noise was giving him the creeps. If he didn't get outside soon, he was going to be in the same shape as the fish. So he rolled down the window.

"Goldfinger never even got to see his new home," mumbled the kid.

He'd spoken so softly that Grady almost didn't hear. But he did. My new neighbors, he thought. And one of them's dead already.

"There's one more fish," said the kid, staring down at the corpse in his hand. "But the cats probably ate it."

"Probably," Grady answered. Then he pushed open the car door.

The cats appeared from nowhere. Hissing and screeching, they vaulted over Grady and leaped out of the car. They flew past Tiny, who was sitting on the sidewalk behaving himself. As Grady told his mother later, the dog couldn't have moved faster if he'd been shot out of a twenty-two.

Tiny tore across the yard after the cats, his hind feet kicking up clumps of lawn. He chased them up the steps and around the porch, down the steps and around the yard again until the cats spied the giant elm and climbed it. Almost to the top. It was a home video in fast forward.

Grady got out of the car. Tiny was howling like a coon dog. The people by the hydrant were staring up at their cats. The little girl was still wailing, and the street was starting to flood.

No, decided Grady, this wasn't a home video. It was a cartoon. All he had to do was figure out how to change the channel.

He walked across the yard, climbed the front steps, and went into the house. He picked up the telephone and dialed.

"Um, is this the fire department?"

It was.

The man on the phone asked who was calling, and it made Grady want to hang up. What if the fire department thought *he'd* done everything?

"Hello?" said the man. "Are you there?"

Grady listened to the hollering and the barking from outside. He switched the phone to his other ear.

"Yeah, I'm still here. I'm Grady Hunstiger. I want to—I mean, I'm sorry to report a bunch of emergencies in my yard. There's a smashed car and a busted hydrant and some cats stuck up high in our tree. Plus everything's getting soaked. And people are yelling."

"Is this a joke, young man?"

"No, sir. It kinda looks like one, but it isn't. It's a big mess."

The man wanted to know exactly where the big mess was.

"Two eighteen Cooney Avenue," answered Grady. "And I think maybe you're gonna need your ladder truck."

He hung up the phone and went back upstairs to his desk.

P.P.P.S. he wrote at the bottom of Mouse's letter.

Forget what I said about things here not looking too good. They just turned horrible. WRITE BACK FAST!

2

Press, Pop, Splat

The fire truck, two police cars, and the Channel Six Action News van arrived in less than seven minutes.

Grady figured that every kid who lived between the fire station and Cooney Avenue had heard the sirens, because they were all there. He stood on the bottom porch step and watched them ride through the flooding street, their feet hooked around the handlebars of their bicycles. Neighbors stood together on their front lawns. Even Mrs. Quade (who wore two hearing aids) came out to watch the action. The whole thing was downright embarrassing. A circus on the front lawn.

Three more dogs joined Tiny, barking and circling the big elm: Dottie, the dalmatian on Grady's paper route, Wendy-Alice's yippy toy poodle, and a basset that did more barking than circling.

Grady watched his baseball coach, Officer Finley, climb out from behind the wheel of the second police car and wave.

"Hey, Huns-tigger," he drawled. "What's up?" He took off his policeman's hat and rubbed his forehead.

"Them, Coach." Grady pointed to the cats.

They were the big attraction. A high-wire act without a net. They didn't want to be rescued. The louder the dogs barked, the farther out the cats climbed on the branches of the elm.

The breeze blew. The branches swayed. The dogs barked. The cats screeched. The Channel Six cameras rolled.

The fire chief turned off the water. Then he asked for help to round up the dogs.

"I'll do it!" said Grady, because it looked like the cats wouldn't last much longer. What if they fell and somebody blamed Tiny? He could see the newspaper headline: GOLDEN RETRIEVER FOUND GUILTY IN DOUBLE MURDER. Tiny would never survive jail.

"Need some help?' the fish kid asked.

Grady saw the dead goldfish still lying in his hand. Yuck. "No thanks," he answered. Then he went into the house to get the box of Yum-yum dog treats his mother kept under the sink.

They worked. Tiny let Grady coax him into the house, and Coach Finley tied Dottie to the front porch. Wendy-Alice sloshed across the street to pick up her toy poodle. Her earrings swung in perfect time with her ponytail.

"Graaaaad-y!" she called out in her bossiest voice. "You sure messed up this time."

Grady pretended not to hear. He bent down and petted the basset, who was lying on the sidewalk munching, his face in the Yum-yum box.

When the firemen carried the last cat down the ladder, the whole neighborhood cheered. The Channel Six crew packed their gear, and a policeman hollered, "Everything's back to normal!" But as Grady watched the new neighbors open the door of their U-Haul trailer, he doubted anything would be normal again. Good thing he was moving to California.

With the thrill of disaster gone, not to mention the TV cameras, the people began to drift away. Grady leaned against the porch railing and watched the kids speed down the street on their bikes.

"See you on the news!" yelled Kyle and Ian Baker on their exactly alike silver ten-speeds.

Grady blushed at the thought. Being on television was something Mouse had always wanted, not him. He slipped his hand into his back pocket and pulled out the letter. The envelope was wrinkled around the edges, but the stamps were firmly in place. He'd put on two—just to be on the safe side. He stared at Mouse's new address and zipcode. 90230 looked awfully far away.

In the bottom left-hand corner he'd written the word URGENT. It had been one of his better ideas. He didn't want the U.S. mail service to think it was just some stupid kid's letter and take their sweet time about it. And he wasn't going to just hand it to the mailman, either. No, sirree. He was going to put it in the airmail slot at the post office himself. Right after he walked the dalmatian home. The sooner he got the letter mailed, the sooner he'd be surfing with Mouse. Or whatever guys did in California.

He slid the letter back into his pocket and untied Dottie from the railing. Then he started around the side of the house. He was glad to have something to do. Something that would get him away from the invasion of the pumpkinheads.

"Where are you going?"

It was an uncomfortably familiar voice. Grady looked down. The fish kid was kneeling in Mr. Peavey's pansies.

"I'm taking Dottie home," Grady answered, not trying very hard to keep the irritation out of his voice. "Wait a minute. What are you doing down there?"

"Burying Goldfinger."

Grady tapped at the edge of the little garden with his shoe. He saw that between two mashed pansies was a small mound of dirt with a circle of pebbles set around it. He ought to at least try to be pleasant to the kid. It was a funeral, after all. So he said, "Straighten up the flowers when you're done, okay?" Then he gave the dalmatian a rub behind the ear. "Come on, Dottie, let's go."

But the kid hopped up and stood in front of him on the sidewalk. "I'll come too," he said, and he gave Grady an eager smile. "Just let me tell my mother I'm leaving."

The kid disappeared around the side of the house before Grady had a chance to holler out the no that was in his mind. So much for the world's fastest funeral.

◉　◉　◉

The kid wouldn't shut up. He fired questions at Grady all the way to Fourth Street like he thought Grady was the Welcome Wagon lady or something.

"How long have you lived here?" "How far away is the school?" "What's it like living in a big town?" And Grady didn't remember what else.

"Seven years, two miles, it's okay, and I don't know," answered Grady, and he speeded up his steps.

"By the way, I'm Burgess Dockerty. I'm eleven."

Burgess?

"You're Grady, right? My mom told me we're going to be living in the same house. I've never lived next door to a friend before."

Grady shot the kid a glare. Friend? What was he talking about?

"We're from Walding," said Burgess. "Ever heard of it?"

Grady shook his head. Maybe Walding wasn't a town. Maybe it was a planet. Way out there, past Pluto someplace.

"It's in Iowa. It's so small it's almost not there." The kid laughed as if he'd made a joke. "I think you already met my sister Laurel. She's three. My big brother Dewey—you know, the one who hit the hydrant? He's in high school. Anyway, my dad got a new job, so here we all are."

Whoopee.

"Where does your dad work, Grady?"

Grady gave Dottie's leash a quick pull and speeded up his steps even more.

"So? Where does he work?" Burgess asked again, hustling to keep up.

"Nowhere. He died."

"Gee. That's too bad. Was he sick? Or was it like a car crash or something?"

Grady felt his temper bubble. Who was this kid anyway? Mister Twenty Questions?

"Look, Burgess. My dad got sick and he died, but everything's fine now."

"But I bet you miss him."

"I don't even remember him. It was a long time ago. When I was a baby. Me and Mom and Tiny are a family now, just the three of us, and we all like it fine. Except

I'm real busy. Maybe we could talk some other time. Okay?"

He gave the kid a small wave and turned down Johnson Boulevard. A chipmunk scooted out of his way. Dottie strained to chase it.

"Sure, Grady." Burgess scooted like the chipmunk and came up alongside. He flashed Grady a smile and said, "We'll just walk. My brother Dewey tells me I talk too much too."

Grady gave Dottie's leash another small tug. Obviously the kid couldn't take a hint. Now what was he supposed to do? Come right out and say, I don't have time to know you, fella. And even if I did, I wouldn't want to. *Pow!* Grady wished. Right in the glasses.

As they walked down the boulevard, Grady made pictures in his head of Burgess lying on the ground with his glasses busted and his front teeth knocked out. Unable to speak another word. Or ask another question.

But Grady's mother kept appearing at the edge of the pictures, so Grady erased them. Instead, out of the corner of his eye he watched the kid. There was something goofy about him. Something besides the motormouth and the battery-operated smile. It took him a minute to figure it out.

The kid didn't walk right. That was it. He didn't walk—he bounced. Like there were Slinkys under his shoes. Grady walked, Dottie pranced, and Burgess bounced. But at least he'd stopped yakking.

They passed Rigotto's Family Restaurant, where Grady and his mother ate pizza on Friday nights. They passed Neal's Service Station, with the air hose that everybody used to pump up their bike tires. But Grady didn't point these out to Burgess. The kid might think he was trying to be friendly.

They turned onto Maple Avenue, and Dottie's tail wagged. She was close to home.

"I like your baseball jersey. I like the way it has your name on it, above your number. Did you get to pick it yourself, the number seventeen? Probably not, huh? Dewey didn't get to pick his number either." The words rushed from Burgess like air from a tight balloon.

Cripes.

"Dewey plays baseball too, you know. He's a pitcher."

In spite of himself, Grady wondered if Dewey was any good and if he was going to play in Johnson Falls. But he didn't ask. He wasn't going to get involved with any of them. He was moving to California.

"I practice with Dewey a lot," Burgess rattled on. "Wanna play catch sometime?"

"NO," Grady answered, louder than he'd meant. "It's just that, like I said, I'm awful busy right now."

Then he pointed to a house with vines that wrapped around it like octopus legs. "This is where Dottie lives," he said. And because it was over now, and he *was* usually a polite person, he added, "Thanks for coming along."

Burgess's face beamed. "No problem. I'll wait here for you."

Geez.

Grady turned and strolled around behind the house. He took his time. He needed to think. He put Dottie in the backyard and closed the fence gate. By peeking through the feathery shrubs that grew on the side of the house, he could see Burgess waiting for him on the sidewalk.

He had to get rid of the kid. Because the last thing he needed right now was a Burgess hanging around. He pulled a small red berry from a shrub and pressed it between his thumb and index finger until it popped. The juice dribbled down his thumb.

After all, he had things to do. Private things. Like mailing Mouse's letter. And he had things to figure out. Like how he was going to explain his brainstorm to his mother. And he had things to picture. Like the white house in California with the palm trees. He and Mouse could play catch under those trees.

He pulled off another berry. Press, pop.

What if he, Grady Hunstiger, just snuck off and left Burgess there? Could he do that? He was almost sure the kid could find his way home. Maybe then he'd figure out that Grady wasn't interested in being friends. And if he left right now, and ran all the way, he could probably make it to the post office before the morning mail left. So ditching Burgess would really do two important things at once.

He was on his third berry and about to make a decision when a car drove into the driveway and Dottie started barking.

"Dottie! *Baby!* Where have you been?" The woman behind the wheel flew out of the car toward the backyard. She charged past Grady, and right behind her came Burgess. Grinning.

"Hey, Grady. I guess we can go now, huh?"

Press, pop, splat.

3

The Smartest Brainstorm Ever

Grady combed his hair and tied his shoelaces, and then, while his mother set the table, he even washed his hands with soap. Without being asked. Because it was going to be an important dinner. A Grady-you're-a-genius dinner. And everything needed to be perfect.

He wiped his hands on the dishcloth and sat down at his usual place. All he had to do now was wait for the right moment to tell his mother about moving to California. It was the smartest brainstorm he'd ever had. She was going to be thrilled.

She was serving brussels sprouts, which was not a good start. She put four of them on his plate, and he watched them roll around like marbles until they came to a stop at the rice. When her back was turned, he picked up the biggest one and slipped it under the table. Tiny, who was not fooled, let it drop to the floor.

"I'm sorry I missed all the excitement today," said his mother as she sat down and put her napkin in her lap. She still had on her nurse's uniform with the shiny gold pin that said GWEN HUNSTIGER, R.N.

"It's a good thing the boy from next door came over to tell me you were on television," she added, "or I would have missed that, too."

Grady tapped one of the three remaining brussels sprouts with his chicken drumstick and watched the green juice trickle out.

"Please don't play with your food, Grady."

"Sorry." He stabbed the sprout with his fork and forced himself to bite through the leafy layers.

"What did the boy say his name was?"

Grady looked up from his plate. "Burgess something."

"Oh, yes. Burgess Dockerty." She pulled a piece of white meat from her chicken. "They seem like such nice people."

Grady was amazed at how dumb a nurse could be sometimes. But then, she hadn't seen the Dockertys in action . . . yet.

"They're a mess, Mom."

He ought to know. As if the morning disaster hadn't been enough, he'd been listening to them bang around on the other side of the center wall for two hours. Thudding up the stairs. Slamming their screen door every five seconds. It had been hard to plan his speech to his mother with all that noise.

He scooped some rice onto his spoon.

"Everybody's a little disorganized on moving day, dear." His mother smiled at him. "And please use your fork."

Grady put down his spoon, even though it didn't make a lot of sense to eat rice with a fork. As he expected, some of it fell in his lap, some of it on the floor. Tiny took care of the floor.

"Why didn't you come down and talk to Burgess when he rang the bell? He seemed awfully friendly."

Grady shrugged and then took another jab at the rice.

"Awfully friendly" didn't begin to cover it. Grady figured it would take Industrial Strength Raid to faze a pest like Burgess. Why, he hadn't been able to shake him until after lunch. The kid had even had the nerve to ask if he could borrow a peanut-butter sandwich. Because their kitchen wasn't unpacked yet, he'd said. And as if that wasn't bad enough, the morning mail was long gone by the time Mouse's letter finally made it to the post office.

Grady picked at the drumstick on his plate. He didn't want to think about Burgess anymore. Or talk about him. The kid didn't matter anyway. It was time to talk to his mother about the important stuff. Like packing up and moving out. He set his fork down next to his plate.

"Mom," he said in his most grown-up voice.

"Yes?"

"I think we should move to California. You could get a job where you wouldn't have to work so hard, and we could live by the Stotts. Just like we did here. Then Mouse and Tiny and I could be together and everything would be all right again."

Phew.

But his mother didn't exactly look thrilled. So he kept going, the way he'd practiced it. "I bet they need lots of nurses in California. You could take care of movie stars when they got sick. And go to Disneyland whenever you wanted. And Grandma could visit us. She likes movie stars too. Plus you wouldn't have to worry about me when you're working, because I'd stay with the Stotts. Like I used to."

His mother rubbed her hand along the back of her neck, and Grady could tell she was tired. He was glad he'd started off with the part about her not having to work so hard in California. He smiled hopefully and launched into the last bit of his speech.

"Mom, this is the best idea I ever had. Me and Tiny, we both vote yes." He nudged Tiny with his knee, and immediately the retriever stood and rested his chin on the table next to Grady. "You don't have to vote right away, Mom. You can think about it."

His mother reached across the table and touched his arm in that way she always did right before she gave him medicine. The brussels sprout in his stomach did a flip-flop.

Was she voting already?

"Grady," she said. "I know you miss Mouse. But give yourself a little time to adjust. Moving to California isn't the answer."

"But, Mom—"

She held up her hand to stop him.

"I know this is hard for you, dear," she went on. "But when things change, you have to let them. If you don't, if you try to hang on, you'll be unhappy that much longer. What you need to do now is make the best of things *here*."

"Won't you just think about it, Mom? You don't have to decide now."

"No."

"Please?" His voice wavered.

"No, Grady. Our lives are here. In Johnson Falls."

"But, Mom—"

"No buts this time, Grady."

"But—"

"No. I'm sorry."

Her voice was soft but firm, and Grady knew she

meant it. He could hardly believe his smartest brain-storm ever had fizzled so fast.

She gave his arm a gentle squeeze and got up to clear away her dishes. The lacy curtains over the kitchen window billowed in the warm breeze.

"I've invited Burgess's mother over for shortcake and coffee tonight, and I'd like you to be here. Now that would be a step in the right direction. You could help the new neighbors feel welcome."

She spoke to him over her shoulder, and Grady could see the steam rise up from the sink as she filled it with hot soapy water.

He suddenly felt very heavy. He picked up his dishes and carried them to the sink in slow motion. Then he set them on the counter.

"I can't," he said without looking into his mother's eyes. "I forgot to tell you. We've got an extra baseball practice tonight."

He held his breath. His mother could usually smell a lie even over the telephone, not to mention seeing one when it stood right next to her. But she didn't say a word until he turned to leave.

"Grady," she called through the steam. "Just one thing."

"What?"

"Pick up the brussels sprout from under the table. The one Tiny wouldn't eat."

● ● ●

It was nearly dark when Grady and Tiny walked home from the ball field. They'd watched the girls' team, the Angels, massacre their opponents 9–2. Wendy-Alice played a mean shortstop, although Grady would never tell her so. She'd seen him during the fourth inning, which meant he'd had to leave his seat in the bleachers and watch the rest of the game from under a tree. He couldn't afford to have Bossyface think he didn't have anything better to do than watch her show off. If only Mrs. Dockerty hadn't come over for coffee. He could have just stayed home and watched TV. Forever.

He pushed the backyard gate open with his mitt. The silhouette of the house loomed up against the dusky sky.

Coming home usually made him feel happy. The old house was a gentle giant that he and Mouse had crawled in, climbed on, swung from, and bored holes through for almost seven years. And its lumbering bigness had always kept them safe. But all that was over now.

He snapped his fingers for Tiny and closed the gate. Fireflies blinked through the air. He stuffed his mitt under his arm, slipped his fingers under the tied-to-gether laces of his cleats, and lifted them off his shoulder. He hadn't used them, of course, but he had to make it look good.

He climbed the back steps and reached for the handle on the screen door. The aroma of coffee and the sound of voices drifted out from the kitchen.

"This shortcake is delicious, Gwen."

Grady's hand froze on the door handle. It was Mrs. Dockerty. He thought she'd be gone by now.

He should open the door. He should go in and hang up his cleats in the hall and walk into the kitchen and say hello. But his hand wouldn't move.

"Yeah, Mrs. Hunstiger. It's real good."

Cripes. Burgess was in there too. Couldn't the kid stay home for once?

"I sure could eat more of this," said Burgess.

"Now, dear," said Mrs. Dockerty.

"That's all right, Burgess," Grady heard his mother say. "I do have more, but I'm saving it for Grady. It's his favorite."

Good ol' Mom. Grady relaxed his fingers and let go of the handle. The cake would be sitting on the counter waiting for him in a blue soup-bowl, like always, the berries hiding under a heap of whipped cream. He could almost taste it.

"On second thought," his mother was talking again, "Grady might have stopped at the Dairy Queen. Let's wait another few minutes and see."

So much for good ol' Mom. Grady chewed at his lip as he stood listening to the clinking of spoons. Was he going to just stand out there in the dark and let Burgess take over his kitchen? And eat his shortcake, too?

He was reaching for the door handle again when Mrs. Dockerty said, "I think your idea is simply wonderful, Gwen. I'm sure Burgess does too."

What idea? What were they talking about?

The thought that his mother had an idea that Burgess would like gave Grady an uncomfortable feeling in the bottom of his stomach. He wanted to call out, "Excuse me! Could you repeat that?" But he couldn't, of course. That was the bad thing about eavesdropping. You had to fill in the blanks.

He set his cleats down quietly on the milk box and pressed his ear against the screen. The shortcake could wait one more measly minute.

"All Burgess needs is someone to show him around," said Grady's mother. "And I think I just might know the right person for the job."

Grady rolled his eyes. He could just bet what was coming next.

"You see," his mother continued, "this isn't an easy time for Grady, either, since the Stotts moved out of your house."

What?

"Their son Matthew was his best friend," she finished.

"Oh?" said Mrs. Dockerty.

"Really?" said Burgess.

Grady sagged against the door frame. How could his mother talk about private things—his things—in front of the Dockertys? In front of Burgess? And how could she say Mouse *was* his best friend?

Is that what she meant when she said things change? That he and Mouse weren't best friends anymore?

"In other words," said Mrs. Dockerty. "If Grady would help Burgess get acquainted, it could be the best thing for both of them."

"Yes," his mother answered. "I certainly think so."

"And, Gwen, if there's anything I can do for Grady while you're at work . . ."

Grady felt sick. He turned his back to the screen door and let his mitt slide off his hand. He looked out into the dark of the backyard.

At least now he knew why his mother had squelched his brainstorm. She didn't understand about change at all. Or best friends. She didn't even understand about him. The new neighbors were more important to her than he was.

"Say, Burgess, do you play baseball?" It was his mother again.

"Just at home with Dewey. But I'm real good, Mrs. Hunstiger."

"Well, there just might be a place for you on Grady's team. Wouldn't that be nice!"

Grady stepped away from the door. He'd heard

enough. He'd lost his appetite, too. Burgess could have his shortcake. Maybe it would give him gas.

Quietly, Grady tiptoed down the steps. At the end of the yard, stretched between two maple trees, was the hammock. He sank into it.

Tiny came to him, carrying the baseball mitt in his mouth. Grady nuzzled him, and let the dog's breath warm his face. Then he stuck the mitt behind his head for a pillow and looked up at the stars.

"We're leaving, Tiny," he said, although he didn't know exactly when he'd decided. "Just you and me. As soon as we hear from Mouse."

And it shouldn't be too awfully long. A week maybe. Enough time to make plans. To get ready. A week to put up with Burgess. He could do it. He might even try to be nice to the kid, so his mother could see that he'd tried to make the best of things—her way.

A firefly hovered above Grady's foot, blinking like a dot on a computer game. He watched it loop and circle and dart away.

So he and Tiny would have to go without her. But before they left, Grady would write her a letter and pin it up on the bulletin board. A letter that would explain everything. She could read it as many times as she wanted, until she understood.

He'd be sure to point out that they were going to California for her, too. To check out the territory. He and Tiny would be like pioneers, brave and resourceful. His mother always admired resourcefulness. He'd tell her he loved her and he missed her, but that he was just doing what he had to do. Making the best of things—his way.

And once they arrived, he'd call her. She'd tell him how sorry she was. She'd say, "You were right, Grady." He'd say, "Thank you." Then she'd say, "You're very brave and resourceful, Grady." And he'd thank her again. Then she'd say, "I'm packed and leaving today." And he'd say, "Good ol' Mom." Nobody would ever mention the Dockertys again.

Tiny climbed gingerly into the hammock, and Grady put his arm around him.

"Everything's gonna be okay, Tiny," he whispered. "We just have to do it ourselves, is all."

4

Think Positive

The most important thing now, Grady decided as he folded Mrs. Quade's morning newspaper and placed it in Tiny's waiting mouth, was the money. How much was it going to cost him to get to California? And how much—exactly—did he have?

He watched Tiny trot up Mrs. Quade's front walk and then gently drop the paper on her welcome mat. Brilliant dog trick number nine. Grady smiled to himself. Another one of Mouse's ideas in action.

He reached into the pocket of his canvas carrier bag and pulled out another paper. Tiny met him on the sidewalk.

"Good boy," Grady said, looking into the retriever's tigery eyes. "Here's another one."

They worked their way down one side of the block

and up the other, Tiny doing his reverse-retrieve, Grady thinking about the money.

What if bus tickets were expensive? He hadn't thought of that when he wrote the letter to Mouse. All the times his grandmother had come from Cincinnati on the bus, he'd never thought to ask her how much it cost. What if he didn't have enough? What if Mouse said yes and Coach Finley said, "We'll miss you, Hunstiger," and he pinned the note for his mother on the bulletin board and then he couldn't pull it off?

The possibility made him feel antsy. His neck started to itch. He gave Tiny another folded newspaper.

Think positive. Isn't that what grown-ups were always saying? He'd seen it too—on a bumper sticker. On that old pick-up that got towed into Neal's Service Station because the engine had blown. Well, never mind that. Think positive.

He switched the strap of the bag to his right shoulder and waited for Tiny to deliver the last paper. Somebody down the street had turned on their sprinkler already, and it made the whole neighborhood smell green. It was a good smell. It was a positive smell. Grady took a deep gulp of it and let it go all the way down to his toes. Then he pulled out the dog treat he'd put in the side pocket of the bag and held it in front of Tiny.

"I want you to think positive," he said. "Like me."

Tiny sat down expectantly and Grady gave him the treat.

"I'm not Richie Rich, you know, but I'm not broke, either. We've got my Christmas money and the money from my route that I was saving for a bike and the pennies upstairs in the coffee can. Not counting the pennies—because I haven't yet—we've got almost fifty dollars, which is not exactly peanuts. Plus, you can ride free, like the dog on Grandma's bus."

Tiny had crunched the dog treat into several pieces and was eating them off the sidewalk.

"Remember when she told us about that dog, Tiny? He got to sit right next to his master the whole trip. That means we can be together all the way. Tiny? Are you listening to me?"

Crunch, crunch.

Grady gave Tiny a pat on the head. Grandma had said something else, too—about that other dog. But he couldn't remember what it was.

The first thing Grady noticed when they got home was proof that good things happen to people who think positive. His mother's car was gone. That meant she'd already left for work, which meant he could get right down to business. California business.

The second thing he noticed, having left for his route from the back door, was proof that thinking positive doesn't mean *all* your troubles will go away.

His front lawn, which had always been a regular, everyday front lawn, looked like the inside of a giant dumpster. Grady wondered if the Dockertys had managed to get any of their belongings inside the house.

Picking the clearest path, he climbed over a pile of dented packing boxes, a set of badminton rackets, and a roofless dollhouse. Good thing he'd soon be leaving. A guy would get sick of this in a real hurry.

When he reached the porch steps, he saw Laurel watching him from inside the Dockerty's front window. Next to her, on the sill, sat the cats. Their green eyes blinking.

Grady wished they'd all just stay there. Indoors and out of trouble. He slapped the carrier bag over his left shoulder and climbed the steps two at a time. "Come on, Tiny. Let's hurry, before they escape."

He was about to open his front door when Burgess bounced out.

"Hi ya, Grady. You got a paper route, huh? Maybe I could help you sometime."

Grady pulled open the door and put one foot in. Share his route? Like he used to do with Mouse? Not in this century. But he was going to try to be nice, he reminded himself. So he said, "I'll see, Burgess. Thanks."

"What are you gonna do now?"

"Eat." Grady pulled Tiny in after him and let the door slam. Man, this nice routine wasn't going to be easy. Even if it was only for one week.

◉ ◉ ◉

Grady found the three-pound Folger's coffee can full of pennies in the back of his bedroom closet. He lugged it down the stairs and set it on the kitchen table. One thing was for sure. Three pounds of pennies were a lot heavier than three pounds of coffee.

He poured himself a glass of juice and put a cinnamon Pop Tart into the toaster. Then he flipped open the Johnson Falls telephone book.

It was not a simple task. Telephone books were not easy to read, no matter what they said in commercials. Grady searched the entire *B* section, which was more reading than he'd done all summer, only to find out that "bus" wasn't even listed there. It was under the *G*s, for Greyhound. By the time he found the number for the downtown station, the aroma of hot cinnamon filled the kitchen. So he took the Pop Tart out of the toaster and ate while he dialed. Tiny sat in front of him in beg position.

"Thank you for calling Greyhound. This is Audrey. May I help you?"

Grady chewed the pie-crusty bits of tart as fast as he

could, and swallowed. Was he supposed to call her Audrey?

"Hello? May I help you?"

If he didn't say something, she was going to hang up. He set the Pop Tart down on the phone book and cleared his throat. But Tiny made a lunge for it, so he picked it back up.

"How much does a ticket to California cost, um, Audrey?"

"Would you be leaving from Johnson Falls, sir?"

"Oh, ah, sure."

"What is your destination in California?"

Grady knocked his fist on the side of his head. Wake up, dumbo!

"Culver City." He broke off a corner of the Pop Tart and gave it to Tiny.

"We don't have a depot in Culver City, sir."

"You don't?"

"No."

"Then how do people get there from here?"

Audrey chuckled. "Your destination would have to be Santa Monica or downtown Los Angeles."

"Oh." Idiot of the universe! He didn't even know where he was going.

"Which would it be, sir?"

Grady could hear Audrey breathing as she waited for him to speak. It reminded him of his teacher Miss

Lilyman, who used to stand in front of the whole fifth-grade class breathing like that while she waited for him to think of an answer.

"How about Los Angeles? How much would that be?"

"One way or round trip, sir?"

Grady chewed at his thumbnail. He should have practiced this before he called Audrey. She asked so fast, he hardly had time to think. But he was just leaving and not coming back, right? So that would be just one ticket. "One way," he answered.

"Just a moment."

He could hear her tapping on the computer keys, and in a few seconds she was back on the line. She gave him the price. But the connection must have gotten goofed up or else his ear was plugged, because it sounded like she'd said "one hundred" something.

He stuck his little finger in his ear to feel for wax. "Could you say that again, please?"

She repeated it.

He nearly dropped the phone. He'd heard right the first time. The ticket would cost way over a hundred dollars including tax. No wonder Grandma rode the bus to visit them only once a year!

"In case you're interested, Santa Monica is the same price, sir. And it's closer to Culver City. I think that's where you'd want to go."

No, he wasn't interested. He wiped his nose with the back of his hand. So much for his smartest brainstorm ever.

"Sir? Is there something wrong?"

He started to speak, but his words were only a squeak, so he took a sip of juice. "It's just that it's too much money. For me, I mean. Even if the tax is included. It's too much."

"Is this ticket for you, sir?"

"Yes."

"How old are you, if I may ask?"

"Eleven. So you don't have to call me 'sir.' My name is Grady."

"Well then, Grady." Audrey's voice perked up. "Children under twelve ride at a greatly reduced price."

"They do?" He wiped his nose again and tried not to hope.

"A one-way ticket for you would be . . ."

He held his breath.

"Sixty-one dollars. Does that help?"

Grady tried to swallow a hiccup. "It might. You see—*hic!*—it all depends on how many pennies there are in the coffee can."

"And if there are enough pennies, Grady, I assume you're not thinking of traveling alone."

Grady broke the rest of his Pop Tart in half and gave it to Tiny.

"Oh, no. I would never make a long trip like that alone."

"Fine. Good luck to you, then, Grady."

"Good luck to you, too, Audrey."

Grady hung up the telephone. Slowly he rose from the chair. The pennies. Everything depended on the pennies. He took a large, positive breath and turned to face the most important coffee can in the world.

And there stood Burgess, a curious grin on his face.

"Hi ya, Grady. Whatcha doin'?"

5

Your Man on the Street

Grady stuck his fists on his hips and scowled at Burgess. It was his best imitation of Miss Lilyman. But Burgess didn't seem to notice. He waltzed into the kitchen anyway, as if Grady had given him a written invitation. Tiny leaped up to greet him like they were old friends.

Big help.

"So who let you in?" Grady demanded.

"Me," Burgess answered, and he patted the front of his green Walding Warriors T-shirt. "You didn't hear me when I hollered to you."

"You allergic to doorbells, too?"

Burgess laughed.

The kid was beyond dense. Grady began to tap his foot against the floor. Tap, tap, tap. But his shoes didn't sound angry, like Miss Lilyman's, so he stopped. He tried to remember exactly what he'd said on the phone. What Burgess the pest could have overheard.

"Just how long have you been here?" Grady raised his voice.

Burgess was petting Tiny, who'd sprawled on the floor for a stomach rub. "Not very long." He shrugged. "Where are you going, anyway? Did I hear you say Los Angeles?"

The questions hung in the air, and Grady felt his mouth go dry. Think, Hunstiger, quick!

"Going someplace? Me? Whatever gave you that idea?"

Burgess looked puzzled. He stood up and smoothed the front of his shirt. "Then who's Audrey?"

"Audrey who?"

"The Audrey you were talking to on the phone?"

"What phone?"

Burgess pointed to the coffee can that stood between them, like evidence, on the table.

"Are those the pennies?"

Grady smiled sweetly. Like Wendy-Alice did, right before she kicked you in the shins. "Pennies? What pennies?"

Burgess rubbed at his ear. He pushed up his glasses. A couple of times he opened his mouth like he was going to say something, but then he slammed it shut.

Grady sighed with relief. Now all he had to do was

remove the coffee can before Burgess decided to pull off the lid and see for himself.

"Was there something you wanted, Burgess?" he asked politely as he reached for the can and slid it to the edge of the table. "A peanut-butter sandwich maybe?"

Grady lifted the can carefully, not wanting Burgess to see how heavy it was. Then he set it in the cupboard and closed the door.

"I get it," Burgess said. "You've got a secret, don't you?"

"No."

"Yeah, you do. You look just like Bunky Peters did after I caught him putting sugar in the gas tank of his dad's car."

Grady was about to say "Who cares?" when it dawned on him that maybe, if he could get Burgess talking about Bunky Whoever-he-was, he'd forget about Los Angeles. And Audrey. And the coffee can full of pennies. It was worth a try.

"Who was Bunky? A kid in Iowa?"

Burgess nodded. "His dad was the mayor. Want to hear about it?"

"You betcha," answered Grady, and he pointed at a kitchen chair. "Have a seat."

Burgess climbed over Tiny, who'd fallen asleep, and plopped down in the chair.

"Want some juice?"

"Sure."

Grady turned to the refrigerator. He thought about the pennies that were sitting in the can that was sitting in the cupboard. Sitting and waiting for him. What he wanted more than anything was to just dump them out on the table and start counting. Would it be California yes? Or California no?

But he couldn't risk it. People with plans had to be patient. So he forced himself to smile when he set the glass of juice down on the checked placemat in front of Burgess. The pennies would have to wait. Besides. It was a nice thing he was about to do. Listen to the new neighbor. Too bad his mom couldn't see this. He sat down at the table with his back to the cupboard.

"Go ahead, Burgess. Tell me everything you know. I've got five minutes."

"First off." Burgess took a swallow of juice. "I was the only person in Walding who knew Bunky did it. Everybody else thought it was Ralph Otto."

"Why?"

"Because when things like that happened in Walding, it usually was Ralph. Once, he booby-trapped the church doors so when Pastor Wilson opened them, a pail of water tipped over on him. I saw the whole thing. Ralph got into big trouble for that one."

"How come you saw this stuff?"

"I was out a lot. Watching and listening. Doing research."

"Doing what?"

"Research."

In spite of himself, Grady was curious. He ran his finger along the ruffled edge of the placemat. "Research for what?"

"My newspaper."

"You had your own newspaper?"

"Yup. It was called *Your Man on the Street*, which was of course me. So I had to do research to find out what was going on. Things seem to happen when I'm around."

Grady wasn't about to argue with that.

"My dad says I have a knack."

Whatever that meant, Grady wasn't going to argue with that, either. "What did you put in the paper?"

Burgess gave him an odd look. Like maybe he thought Grady'd asked a dumb question. "I put in the news, Grady. You know, what's happening. That's what a newspaper is."

Grady shifted around in his chair. "I knew that."

"I found out what people were doing and saying, and then I wrote about it."

"How'd you print it up?"

"On a machine at my dad's work. A hundred copies in minutes. It was simple."

Grady tipped his chair back and looked at Burgess. As usual, his glasses were lopsided, and his orange hair stuck up like he'd gotten real scared by something. A guy would never guess, just by looking at him, that he had any brains at all. But having your own newspaper? That was a pretty good idea. Even he, Grady, and Mouse had never thought of that one.

"Did you sell any?"

"Sure. I sold lots. Made money, too. I was saving for a video camera. So I could make movies."

"Why'd ya quit?"

"We moved."

"Oh, yeah. Right."

"Plus, I ran into a few problems."

"Like what?"

"Like when Bunky socked me in the face. My glasses haven't worked right since."

"You put *that* in the paper? About him messing with his dad's car?"

Burgess set his juice glass down on the table with a clack. "Sure. Newspaper reporters get in trouble all the time for telling the truth. But some things are too big to be secrets. Know what I mean?"

Grady looked down at the green and white checks on the placemat. He knew exactly what the kid meant. That the next week was going to be horrible. Not only was he going to have to hide everything he was doing from his mother, now he had to worry about "Your Man on the Street" spying on him from next door. At least he'd gotten him off the track this time.

Grady pushed his chair away from the table and

stood up. It was time to get the kid out of the house . . . and keep him out. "I've got stuff to do, Burgess."

"Can I help?" Burgess climbed over the back of his chair to avoid bumping Tiny, who was snoring.

"No, thanks."

"Can I go to baseball practice with you? My mom said your mom said it was tonight."

Grady wanted to say no. But wouldn't this be just the thing he needed to show his mom that he was trying to make the best of things?

"Okay. Five o'clock. Be ready."

Burgess beamed. "Thanks, Grady." Then he walked out of the kitchen and headed for the front door. "About your secret," he hollered from the living room. "It's safe with me."

Then the front door banged shut and he was gone.

Safe? What did safe mean to a kid who ratted on everybody in town? Grady banged his fist on the counter. And here he'd thought the kid had forgotten!

"Relax, Hunstiger," he whispered. "Stop and think. How much does Burgess know?

Not much, really. Only the big thing. That he had a secret.

Geez.

Grady squatted down next to Tiny. "He's just like you when you play tug, Tiny. He doesn't want to let go."

But at least when Tiny had one of his shoes, or a

sock, Grady could dangle a dog treat in front of him or say, "Drop it, Tiny!" and he would. Burgess wasn't going to be that easy.

Grady ran his hand over the retriever's near-white belly fur. He'd have to figure out something real special for Burgess. Something that would make him drop it like a hot potato. But what? He'd think on it later. After he counted the pennies.

6

California Dreamin'

Grady locked the front door, the back door, and, to be on the safe side, the door to the cellar. He pulled down the blinds in the living room and shut the curtains in the kitchen, and when he was finally satisfied that he could not possibly be spied on, he climbed the stairs to his bedroom to hunt up his savings.

He dug through the middle drawer of his dresser. Past the baseball cards, the nose plugs, the Snickers wrappers, the cap gun, until his fingers touched his Christmas stocking. As he pulled it out, the bells his grandma had knit into the red stripe at the top jingled. It was a good sound. He held up the stocking in front of his face. The folded dollar bills made a nice bulge in the toe. He smiled. The knitted Santa face smiled back. Now *that*, he thought, was a smile you could trust.

He slid down the banister and walked back to the kitchen, shaking the stocking all the way. At the sound of the bells, Tiny woke up from his nap. Grady gave him a pat as he brushed past. Finally he could get down to business.

◉ ◉ ◉

There was only $41.00 in the Christmas stocking. He'd thought for sure there'd be at least fifty. But then he'd bought a few things. Like candy. And the autograph book for Mouse. And a little more candy. Grady looked at the thin stack of bills and wished he didn't like candy quite so much. Now he needed twenty more dollars, and that was an awful lot of pennies.

With hope he pulled off the lid of the coffee can and dumped.

The pennies covered the kitchen table and spilled onto the floor. There were hundreds of them. Maybe even thousands. Grady scooped a handful and let the coins slip through his fingers. He felt like a king.

And there weren't just pennies. Quarters, nickels, and dimes had come tumbling out of the coffee can too. Plus Superman. His miniature, plastic Superman. The cape long gone, the big *S* on his chest scratched almost completely off, Superman was the last thing that had poured out in the gush of coins. Grady picked him up, remembering the time he and Mouse had thrown him out of the attic window—to see how far they could make him fly.

He hadn't done too well. Must have been some kryptonite around, they'd figured, so they'd stuck him back in the coffee can to recover.

Grady set Superman on the toaster to watch over the counting. For luck. Now he was ready.

He arranged the pennies in stacks of ten. Each time he had ten stacks, he gently pushed them together into groups. Dollar groups.

Twice the doorbell rang. He didn't answer it. Once the telephone rang. He didn't answer that, either. He could hear the Dockertys bumping around on the other side of the center wall for a while, but then their front door slammed, and from then on it was all quiet. He skipped lunch. Only once did he stop, and that was to get himself a drink of water and to let Tiny out because he was looking desperate.

When all the pennies were stacked, Grady stood back to size up his work. The counter was covered from one end to the other with what looked like an army of copper robots. It was a powerful sight.

Then he picked up a pencil, tore off a piece of paper from the telephone message pad, and wrote $61.00 at the top. It was the magic number. The amount Audrey had said he would need to buy his ticket.

"Think positive," he said, and he glanced at Superman. Then slowly he began to count his dollar groups, touching each one as he went.

One dollar.

Two dollars.

Three dollars . . .

When he finished, he picked up his pencil and wrote, "Grand Penny Total: $16.38."

Then there were the quarters, and the nickels, and the dimes. He wrote down how much there was of each.

Then he took another quick peek at Superman, and carefully began to add all the numbers he'd written on the paper. As the tip of his pencil touched each one, he said it out loud. He forced himself to go slowly. When he finally finished, he wrote at the bottom of his piece of paper: $64.58.

"A WRIIIIIIGHT!"

He whooped and he twirled himself in circles. He gave Superman a salute and he bowed to the penny army. Then he took a big breath and made himself add up all the numbers two more times. Because this math paper had to be right.

It was.

He felt dizzy all over. His fingers tingled from touching all that money. He went into the living room and lay down on the sofa, to let it all soak in. Not only could he buy a ticket to California, he'd have money left over!

He could see the two of them, him and Mouse, at Universal Studios. Having their picture taken with King Kong. He could see them at Disneyland, riding on a ride ... their hair blown back in the wind. He could see them in Hollywood, walking past the homes of the stars. Swimming in the ocean. Covering up Mouse's dad with sand at the beach until only his head stuck out. Grady the Great and the Mighty Mouse. A team again.

He let his thoughts spin, each one turning into the next and the next, until he had to sit up to slow down.

How smart he'd been to think of writing Mouse! He wondered where the letter was now. Probably on a jet—a 747—winging its way west. In only a week he and Tiny would be on their way too. And soon after, his mother would drive out. Then everything would be perfect.

Tiny was barking at the back door. Slowly Grady got up from the sofa to let him in. He felt like he was in a dream. When he opened the door, Tiny made a beeline for his water dish and nearly knocked him over. Grady was about to close the door when he saw a note sticking out of the milk box. It had his name on it.

> *Grady,*
>   *We are going to see my dad's new work.*
>   *We wanted you to come, but I guess you went someplace without me seeing.*

*I will be ready for baseball at 5. I hope I make
the team.*

*Your friend,
Burgess Dockerty
P.S. I won't say anything about you know what.*

Friend, ha. If it wasn't for Burgess, everything would
be smooth sailing now. What a pest.

Grady crumpled up the note and pitched it into the
garbage can. Then he turned to scoop up the pennies
when a thought crossed his mind. He took the note out
of the garbage, uncrumpled it, and read it again. The
part that said *I hope I make the team.*

He looked down at the wrinkled paper in his hand
and smiled. He had an idea. A real special idea. He
leaned against the counter and let his brain kick into
gear. It was time to hatch a bribe.

7

The Bribe

Grady checked the clock on his dresser. It was ten minutes to five. He looked out of his bedroom window and saw Burgess sitting on a packing box—his cap on, his mitt in his lap—ready and waiting.

He went over the bribe plan one more time. Then he walked down the stairs to say good-bye to his mother, who was relaxing in the living room after a long day at work. She took a sip of her tea.

Grady looked at the tired sag of her shoulders. If only she understood about things. If only she'd believed him when he told her how happy she'd be in California. Oh well, it would all happen soon.

"It's nice of you to take Burgess along," she said, her eyes smiling up at him over the rim of her mug.

He shrugged. Now that she had mentioned it, he could pretend it wasn't important. He picked up his baseball cap from the coffee table and put it on backwards, as usual, so the visor was almost touching his neck. "Bye, Mom."

"Bye, dear."

With his cleats hung over his shoulder, his mitt tucked under his arm, and the bribe firmly set in his mind, he opened the screen door and went outside.

Burgess popped up like a jack-in-the-box.

Grady whistled for Tiny.

"Do you think I'll get a uniform, Grady? With my name on it? I wonder what number I'll be."

They started down Cooney Avenue, Burgess talking a blue streak, Grady thinking. Getting himself ready to say what he was going to say to Burgess . . . and what he wasn't.

He thought about Coach Finley. He thought about how, in the three years he'd been on the coach's team, he'd never seen the coach scream at the umpire, or yell at his team, or call somebody stupid. He was even nice to his own son Arthur, who, as catcher, got hit with so many foul tips there was almost nothing left of his mask but dents. And he thought about how Coach Finley never benched a player or turned anybody away who wanted to learn the game. This was part of what he *wasn't* going to tell Burgess.

And then there was the team. The Rigotto Royals.

Yikes, what a mess. The coach said their only problem was their attitude. That they didn't believe they could win a game without Mouse pitching. "Just because you haven't yet," he'd say after every defeat, "doesn't mean you won't soon!" But nobody believed him. They reeked, plain and simple. But Burgess wasn't going to hear about that, either. Because truth was not part of the bribe.

Grady let the leaves from a low-hanging elm branch swish against his face. Why was it, he wondered, that people with plans had to lie so much?

They started over the creek bridge. Tiny leaped off, like always, and Burgess began talking about cleats. Grady decided to interrupt.

"Burgess," he said. "I'm afraid I've got bad news."

Out of the corner of his eye, Grady saw Burgess look over at him.

"I wish there was a nice way to say this, but I can't think of one. So I'll just say it. I don't think you're going to make the team."

Burgess stopped, and Grady had no choice but to stop, too.

"Why not?"

Grady leaned against the bridge railing. He could hear Tiny splashing around underneath him. "Because you don't have any experience."

"I do too have experience. I've played lots of catch and I'm real good. Just ask Dewey."

"I'm not talking about playing catch, Burgess. I'm talking about being on a team. You don't have any team experience. You wouldn't know when to do what. Unfortunately, Coach Finley thinks team experience is everything."

"He does?"

"He does. Coach Finley doesn't waste time with rookies, Burgess."

"He doesn't?"

"No, he doesn't."

"Then why'd you bring me along?"

Grady had expected that one. "So you could meet the guys."

"Oh."

Grady could almost feel Burgess's shoulders slump. He looked down at the creek and watched Tiny bite the water as it bubbled over the rocks.

"The thing is, Burgess, us guys on the team have played together for years. We've got timing. We've got style. We've got rhythm. You probably won't understand this because you've never been on a team, but let me tell you. We're a real machine."

He was laying it on thick and it was mean and he knew it. So he reminded himself that he was only doing what he had to do. But as he talked, he couldn't help thinking of Arthur's dented mask. And Kyle Baker watching airplanes from third base. And Nick Rigotto trying his best to pitch like Mouse but still walking every other batter. The Royals. Some machine.

He dug in his pocket for a piece of bubble gum because his mouth felt like a desert.

"Maybe I could be a bat boy?" Burgess asked in a small voice.

"We don't need one."

Burgess looked like somebody had punched him in the stomach. He sat down on the bridge and let his legs hang over the edge. He turned his head away so Grady couldn't see his face. But he could hear the kid gulping air. Like he was trying not to cry or something.

Geez Louise.

This was not supposed to happen. Every time he'd rehearsed in front of the hall mirror, Grady'd imagined ol' Burgess grinning through the whole thing. How could he have known the kid would take it personally?

Grady kicked at the bottom of the iron railing. It was really the kid's own fault, wasn't it? Sure it was. If he hadn't been so pushy, if he hadn't barged into the kitchen and eavesdropped on a phone call that was none of his business, this wouldn't be happening. The kid could ruin everything. "Just remember that, Hunstiger," he told himself.

He looked down at Burgess. The Walding Warriors' T-shirt he was wearing was at least six sizes too big. It said "Dew" on the back, above a large number fourteen. The letters and the numbers moved up and down with every gulp of air that he took. Grady sat down next to him on the wooden slats of the bridge. He almost put his hand on Burgess's shoulder. Instead he gave him the gum.

"Here. Chew this. You'll feel better."

Burgess stuck the soft purple chunk in his mouth.

Grady watched Tiny wading in the creek. He tried to think about something happy, like how much fun it was going to be in California. Gum would have helped, but he'd only brought the one piece.

He picked at a sliver of wood. Why was he sitting there moping? Wake up, man! It was time for part two of the bribe plan! Part two would put a smile back on the kid's face. He swung his legs back and forth. He felt better already.

"Kid," he said, like an idea had just popped into his head, "maybe I can help you."

Burgess turned and blinked at him. The bubble gum made his one cheek puff out like a squirrel's. The air around him was grapey sweet.

"Help me?"

"Yeah. I think maybe I can get you on the team."

Burgess's eyes got big like moons. "How?"

"I'm going to put in a good word for you with the coach. I'm going to tell him I think you've got potential."

"Really? You'd do that for me?"

Grady nodded.

"Gee, Grady," he said, sniffing in between chews. "Nobody's ever put in a good word for me before."

Good grief. Hadn't the kid ever had a friend? Of course, he didn't now, either, Grady reminded himself. Just somebody pretending to be.

Grady tossed the sliver of wood into the creek and watched it float away. How many times, he wondered, had he and Mouse stuck up for each other? Or put in a good word? Too many to count, that was for sure.

"Grady?" said Burgess.

"What?"

"If I can ever help you, just let me know."

Bingo.

"Thanks, Burgess."

Grady scrambled up and hollered for Tiny, who'd waded downstream. Burgess scrambled up too, like a shadow, and in a minute they were on their way to the field.

"Say, Burgess," Grady said as he shifted his cleats to his other shoulder. "Maybe there is something you can do for me."

"Sure, Grady. Anything."

Grady stopped, turned, and looked Burgess straight

in the eyes. "You know that secret you think I have? The one that's none of your business?"

Burgess scratched at his ear. He blew a large bubble and popped it. And while Grady waited, he turned his baseball cap backwards on his head so that the visor rested on his neck. Then he beamed his biggest smile yet. A real nine-volter.

"What secret?"

Grady sighed. As long as the kid didn't find out anything else, it ought to work. At least for a week.

As they walked down Johnson Boulevard, Kyle and Ian Baker swept past them on their bikes, waving. Their mitts hung from their handlebars.

"Rigotto Royals?" asked Burgess.

"Yup. Third base and center field."

Grady was counting on the fact that Burgess wouldn't know enough to notice how bad the Royals really were. At least not right away. Not until he and Tiny were long gone on the Greyhound bus. But just in case, it wouldn't hurt to say something. So as they neared the field, he told Burgess that a few of the guys were just getting over the measles, and a couple others had been in bed with the flu.

"So if we look a little off this week, Burgess, that's why."

"I know all about the flu, Grady. I had it once. It was terrible. Want me to tell you about it?"

"No thanks. We're almost there."

The field was in sight, and Tiny raced on ahead. Baseball practice, Grady explained, was one of the retriever's favorite activities.

They crossed the boulevard and walked onto the corner of the outfield. Coach Finley was standing on the pitchers' mound, talking to Nick.

Burgess grabbed Grady's elbow. He looked like he'd seen a ghost. "Is *he* the coach?"

"Yeah. Why?"

"He was at our house yesterday. He's the policeman who gave Dewey a ticket for hitting the hydrant."

"So?"

"So what if he recognizes me?"

"So what if he does?"

Burgess didn't seem convinced. He took a couple steps backward, and Grady wondered what the big deal was. Who cared if Coach Finley was a policeman? Everybody knew he was the nicest guy in town.

He looked at Burgess. Oh. Well. Almost everybody . . .

Grady ran his foot back and forth along a crack in the sidewalk. He watched Burgess take another step back. "Listen, Burgess. I'll take care of this for you too. I'll tell Coach you won't cause any more problems. He trusts me."

"Are you sure?"

"I'm positive."

Burgess hesitated. Finally he nodded yes. He promised to wait on the sidewalk while Grady ran up to the pitchers' mound to put in the good word.

"Coach?"

Coach Finley turned around and stuck his clipboard under his arm. "Hey, Hunstiger. What's up?"

"I brought a new kid, Coach. His name is Burgess and he wants to join the team."

Coach Finley looked around to see where Burgess was.

Grady pointed. "He just moved here, and my mom thinks he needs to meet some people. He's never played on a team."

The coach smiled. "Well, get him over here and let's have a look."

"Sure." Grady waved Burgess over, and then stood watching while the kid dragged his heels all the way to the pitchers' mound.

"So this is the rookie, eh?" Coach Finley used his policeman's voice, and Burgess's face went pale again.

"Yes, sir," answered Grady. "This is Burgess Dockerty."

Coach Finley put out his hand and Grady watched Burgess shake it, his fingers disappearing instantly in Coach's big grip.

"What do you think, Hunstiger? Should we put him on the team or should we eat him for lunch?"

Grady heard Burgess suck in his breath. But then Coach Finley laughed.

Maybe, thought Grady, he should have at least told the kid that Coach Finley liked to tease.

"Well, sir," Grady answered, trying to sound benevolent, "I think we should put him on the team."

"Then I guess you're on, Dockerty." Coach gave Burgess a good-hearted slap on the back. "Welcome to the Royals."

8

The Fastball

By the time Coach Finley finally blew his whistle and hollered, "That's all for tonight, fellas!" Grady could almost taste the Butterfinger Blizzard he was going to buy when he got to the Dairy Queen.

He called to Tiny, and the retriever bounded in from center field with one ear flopped back and his tongue hanging out. Grady gave him a pat and then turned to see Burgess get up from behind home plate.

Coach Finley had tried the kid out as catcher, which had delighted Arthur, who said he was sick of wearing the mask anyway, and Burgess hadn't done too badly. Grady had to admit the kid was good with his glove. He'd caught most of Nick's wild pitches, which was semi-miraculous, and his arm was accurate besides. The

Royals looked better than they had for weeks. Well, sort of.

Burgess jogged up to Grady. "I think Coach Finley likes me, even if I am a rookie. What'd you think?"

"You did okay," Grady answered, and then because he'd done his good deed for the day, he said, "See you tomorrow, Burgess."

"Kyle invited me to the Dairy Queen. He said all the guys will be there. Aren't you coming?"

Darn.

◉ ◉ ◉

As usual the Queen was jammed. Most of the Royals had already arrived when Grady and Burgess crossed the street and stood under the revolving Brazier sign. Grady could see them sitting in the grass blowing straw wrappers at each other. The air pulsed with rock music, and bunches of kids milled around the parking lot. A bowling team had taken over the picnic tables.

Grady got in line in front of Burgess, and the creamy smell of soft serve washed over him like a wave. Through the window ahead of him he saw the stainless-steel squirters that dispensed syrups. Next to them lay bins full of toppings: malted-milk balls and broken bits of candy bars, sprinkles, peanuts, and chocolate cookies, too. He was about to reach into his pocket for his money when Wendy-Alice and her sidekick Elizabeth walked up.

"If it isn't Hunstiger," Wendy-Alice snickered. "The neighborhood master of disaster."

"Shut up, Bossyface."

"You don't mind if we get in line with you, do you, Grady?"

"Yeah. I mind."

"Aw, don't be a pill." Wendy-Alice looked behind Grady, at Burgess. "Hey, aren't you the kid who just moved in? The one with the cats?"

"Who, me?" asked Burgess.

"Yeah, you. My Toodles almost had a heart attack because of those cats."

"Toodles is an idiot," said Grady.

"She's a lot smarter than this thing." She pointed down at Tiny.

Grady felt his face start to burn. He edged forward. "Knock it off, Wendy-Alice. Or I'll put some dents in your tin grin."

"*Ooh!* A threat!" She turned to Elizabeth. "Aren't you scared, Bethie?"

"Yeah," said Elizabeth. "Real scared."

"Then leave," said Grady.

They didn't.

"You stink, Hunstiger. You know that?" Wendy-Alice sneered. "But your team stinks worse. The Royals, phew! You guys oughta take lessons from us Angels."

"Yeah," added Elizabeth. "Remedial Baseball."

The girls thought that was funny. They hooted and cheered.

Grady jammed his fists into his pockets. It was hard sometimes, not punching girls.

"We could teach you guys how to play, Hunstiger. Then we could have a little game. We'd call it Baby Baseball."

They thought that was even funnier. *"Baby Baseball! Yeh!"*

Grady could feel Burgess behind him, listening. Waiting for him to say something that would shut her up. The kid didn't know, of course, that shutting up Wendy-Alice was not exactly a piece of cake. In fact, nobody Grady knew had ever done it. But he better at least say something. "Listen, Beanpole. We could wipe the Angels off the face of the earth in one inning."

"Wanna bet?" With a gleam in her eye Wendy-Alice turned and stepped up to the order window, and Grady realized that both girls were now in front of him in the line. When had they done that? He hadn't even noticed. Geez, girls were sneaky.

"Grady." It was Burgess.

"What?"

"Why don't we play her dumb team?"

Grady shook his head. He didn't even want to imagine what would happen to the Royals if they played the Angels, division champions two years in a row. But he couldn't tell Burgess that. So instead he said, "Naw, that'd be too easy."

"Then we could beat her up."

"She's bigger than both of us, Burgess. Plus, I'm not supposed to hit girls."

"Well, I'm not supposed to hit anybody. But we gotta do something."

"Like what?"

Wendy-Alice and Elizabeth swaggered past them then, carrying their cones. "See ya at *Baby Baseball*, geeks!" they said, extra loud.

Burgess leaned over Grady's shoulder. "We gotta get 'em, Grady."

"I know, I know."

◉ ◉ ◉

Grady and Burgess shuffled through the crowd toward the team, balancing their drinks. Kyle and Ian Baker had saved them a spot on the grass, which was right where Grady wanted to be. He needed to talk to Kyle. With both his tire rims bent and his chain busted, he needed Kyle's bike to get his backpack full of pennies down to the bank. He could exchange them for dollar bills, no sweat, and then he wouldn't look like a dope walking into the Greyhound depot with 1,638 pennies. Very resourceful planning. Too bad he couldn't tell his mother.

They sat down, Grady with his Blizzard, Burgess with a giant lime slush. Burgess held out the cup of water they'd gotten for Tiny. The retriever slurped noisily.

"Where'd you learn to catch like that, Dockerty?" asked Kyle.

"You're lots better than Arthur," added Ian. "Maybe we'll start winning some games now."

"You mean you don't always win?" asked Burgess, and Grady nearly choked on his first mouthful of Blizzard. The bribe would never work—even for a week—if Burgess heard stuff like this! Quickly Grady swallowed, and then he changed the subject. "Kyle, could I borrow your bike tomorrow?"

"Depends," said Kyle.

"Violin lessons tomorrow," said Ian, and he scooped up a spoonful of his root-beer float. "So, Grady. What'd ya hear from Mouse?"

Oh, man. Burgess shouldn't hear this, either.

"Nothing," Grady answered, and then he changed the subject again. "What time are your violin lessons tomorrow, Kyle?"

"Who's Mouse?" asked Burgess at the same instant, and the Baker twins looked up from their floats.

"You don't know about Mouse?" they both asked.

Burgess shook his head.

"Your bike, Kyle," said Grady. "I just need it for an hour."

"Geez, Hunstiger," interrupted Ian. "How could you not tell Burgess about the Mouse?"

"Yeah," echoed Kyle.

Grady wanted to bop both the Bakers. Why couldn't they just mind their own business? And why did they have to say everything twice?

"About your bike, Kyle."

"Who *is* the Mouse?" Burgess looked back and forth from Kyle to Ian like he was watching a game of Ping-Pong.

"Just a guy," answered Grady.

"*Just a guy!*" Kyle looked shocked. Grady watched him turn to Burgess, his eyes nearly popping. "Mouse isn't just a guy, Burgess," he said. "He's Grady's best friend."

"They were together all the time," said Ian. "Until Mouse moved."

"To California," said Kyle.

"You're living in his old house," piped Ian.

"And maybe you're even sleeping in his old room," added Kyle.

"Aha!" said Burgess, sounding like he'd just discovered a zillion-dollar bill. He turned to Grady. "Mouse is Matthew Stott, isn't he?"

Grady shoved his spoon down into his cup. He should never have let Burgess come here tonight. Or taken him to practice. Or tried to be nice. If only his mother had stayed out of things, none of this would be happening.

He grabbed his cleats and stood up. The only thing left to do now was get Burgess out of there. Before he started playing "Your Man on the Street" again and forgot all about the bribe.

"We're leaving, Burgess. My mom needs me at home," he lied.

"But I haven't finished my slush."

"Then bring it along." Grady slung the cleats back over his shoulder. "Kyle, can I borrow your bike or what?"

Kyle gave Grady a funny look. "Sure, Grady. But how come you don't go buy yourself a new bike? That piece of junk you've got never works."

"Really," added Ian. "With your paper route, you must have a lot of money."

Sure, he had money. But not for a bike. "Come on, Burgess. Come on, Tiny. Let's go."

Grady turned on his heels and headed for the trash can. When he reached it, he yanked up the lid and whipped the rest of his Blizzard in. He didn't feel like eating a treat anymore.

◎ ◎ ◎

As usual, Burgess talked the whole way home. About the Royals and Coach Finley and how he'd like to be a pitcher someday. But at least he wasn't asking questions.

Maybe, thought Grady, if he ignored the kid, he'd go away. So he started counting the cracks in the sidewalk. One . . . two . . . tree roots . . . three . . .

He was about to step on crack number four, which was just past Mrs. Quade's driveway, when Burgess said "You're going to California to be with Mouse, aren't you? You're running away."

The words came at Grady like a fastball. A fastball that hit him square in the chest and almost knocked him over. *You're running away.*

"No, I'm not."

"Yes, you are."

"No, I'm not!" And he wasn't lying this time. He wasn't running away. He was moving. "But even if I was, it's none of your business. Remember? So drop it."

But Burgess wasn't going to drop it. Not this time. Grady could tell. Because this was one of those secrets too big to keep. "Your Man on the Street" had arrived.

Grady clicked his tongue at Tiny and speeded up his steps. He didn't even need to guess what Burgess would do next. He'd tell his mother. Then Mrs. Dockerty would run next door with the news, and the trip would be history. His mother would be furious, especially if she believed the part about running away. She probably wouldn't let him see Mouse for years, and there wasn't a thing in the world he could do about it, because no bribe was going to work this time. Burgess was going to ruin his life.

"Grady! Wait up!"

Grady didn't. He hurried past the pickets of Wendy-Alice's fence and tried hard not to think about Mouse. He tried even harder not to think about how he missed him at this exact minute right now something terrible.

"Grady," huffed Burgess. "I wanna talk to you."

Grady stopped and spun to face him. His cleats on their long laces swung after him. One shoe rapped him in the back and the other bumped him in the chest.

"Leave me alone, Burgess."

"But, Grady. It is too my business, what you're doing. 'Cause we're friends."

Burgess smiled weakly. A faint green mustache curved above his mouth from the lime slush, and his baseball cap was on backward. Like he thought he belonged.

Grady glared at him. "Friends? Us?"

Burgess's mouth dropped open.

"You don't know the first thing about being friends, Burgess. Not the first thing. You think you can just push your way into a guy's life and that makes you a friend? It makes you a pest. P–E–S–T. *Pest.* You don't even know when to talk and when to *shut up!*"

Grady kept glaring at him. To make sure he finally

got the message. He imagined lasers shooting out from his eyes toward Burgess. Any second now the kid would shrink like the witch in *The Wizard of Oz*, and cry "I'm mellllting!"

But Burgess didn't, of course. No such luck. He just stood there with his eyes round like soup bowls and his mouth hanging open. Like he was waiting for Grady to take it all back. Well, forget that. When you ruin a guy's life, you pay the price.

Grady looked down at Tiny, who'd sidled up next to him. The retriever leaned against him. As Grady touched the silky fur of his head, he realized his hand was shaking.

"Go away, Burgess," he said.

And Burgess did. He walked toward the old house with hardly a bounce. His green T-shirt drooped down past his knees, and not once did he turn around.

9

Out on a Limb

Grady climbed his back-porch steps and sat down on the milk box. He slid his cleats off his shoulder, leaned against the house, and let his breath out long and slow. He needed a minute to cool down . . . and a few more to think things over.

He'd already decided, on the way home, that he wasn't going to let himself think about Burgess's soupy eyes or his sad-sack walk. The kid had deserved getting yelled at. Why, he ought to be grateful Grady hadn't punched him in the glasses like the kid in Iowa did.

"Is that you, Grady?" his mother called to him from the kitchen.

"Yeah, it's me."

"Good. I'll get the cards out."

He'd forgotten it was Tuesday. Gin-rummy night.

"I'll be right in."

He was going to have to tell his mother about his trip, and he was going to have to do it fast. Before Burgess blabbed his mangled version of the story to Mrs. Dockerty and Mrs. Dockerty rushed over with the news. He'd be grounded for the rest of his life.

A mosquito circled above his head, and he took a swipe at it with his mitt. If only he could think of a way to explain things to his mother. A way to make her understand why he'd planned his trip to California even without her permission. How he was really doing it for both of them. Maybe he could even get her to change her mind ... now that she'd had time to get used to the idea. But where to begin?

"Grady! What are you doing out there?"

The mosquito landed on Grady's arm. He watched it settle in, adjusting its wings and legs until they were in just the right spot. He waited until the mosquito was aimed and ready to bite him, and then he flicked it, sending it sailing across the porch. Because pests, if a guy wasn't careful, could eat him alive.

◉ ◉ ◉

When Grady walked into the living room, his mother was sitting on the floor, shuffling the cards.

"How was practice?" she asked without looking up.

"Okay."

"How did Burgess get along?"

"Okay."

"And the Dairy Queen. How was that?"

"Okay."

"Want to cut the cards?" she asked, and set the deck in front of him.

He rapped his knuckles on the top of the deck. "Naw, that's okay."

"Grady!"

"What?"

"Say something besides okay, will you? You sound like a broken record."

"Okay."

She laughed and he laughed with her, as if he'd been doing it on purpose. But the truth was, it was going to be hard to talk and think and play cards at the same time.

He watched her deal the blue-and-white cards into two piles, one for each of them. On the back of every card was a picture of a man wearing wings, riding a bicycle. Why would anybody ride a bike if he could fly?

"Is something bothering you, Grady?"

His mother the mind reader. But he wasn't ready. Not yet.

"No," he answered.

He picked up his cards and fanned them out in his hand. Two kings, three nines, and a possible run of clubs. He drew a card from the top of the deck. The queen of hearts, looking worried, stared up at him. He tossed her onto the discard pile.

Now what was he going to say to his mother? Maybe he should start with how he'd actually been following her advice. When you have a problem, she always said, think it through. Then make the best decision you can. And above all, believe in yourself, no matter what other people say. Well, that's what he was doing, wasn't it?

"You must have quite a hand there, kiddo."

"Huh?" Grady looked up. His mother was smiling at him.

"You've been staring at it for a while now."

"Sorry. Just trying to figure things out."

His mother drew a card and then slid it carefully into the middle of her hand.

Or maybe he should start with the part he knew she'd like. The part about him and Tiny being brave and resourceful . . .

"You know, Grady, I'm proud of you." She dropped the four of clubs. "You did something important today. You gave yourself a chance to make a new friend."

What?

She looked at him and Grady saw her eyes twinkling. Twinkling like when he'd found the five-dollar bill under the booth at Rigotto's and turned it in to the cashier. Oh, no.

"The easiest thing in the world," she continued, "would have been for you to ignore Burgess. You could have spent the whole summer moping around, wishing Mouse was still on the other side of that wall." She nodded her head toward the staircase. "But you didn't do that, Grady. You went out on a limb."

He was out on a limb all right, just like the Dockertys' cats. But it was a different limb than the one she thought he was on, and there wasn't anybody around to help with the rescue part. Now how could he tell her he wanted to leave for California?

"Grady, do you want that four?"

"What? Oh, um, yeah." It was even harder to *listen* and think and play cards at the same time. He picked up the four and stuck it between the three and five. What was the first thing he planned to say again? His brain was getting a little fuzzy. He pulled out the king of spades from his hand to discard, but he looked even more upset than the queen. Grady shoved him back in place and tossed a nine. Mistake!

"What's the matter tonight, O wonderful son?" his mother asked, and it sounded to Grady as if she was teasing only a little.

He wanted to tell her that she had him mixed up with somebody else. That he wasn't very wonderful. That the truth was, he didn't even want to know Burgess, let alone be friends. He wanted to tell her that the old house wasn't fun anymore and he didn't want to live on Cooney Avenue another minute. But most of all, he wanted to tell her that he needed to leave for California soon, because, even though she didn't agree, *that* was making the best of things.

But the phone rang.

"I'll get it, Mom." He dropped his cards on the floor and leaped up. He should have told her when he had the chance! Now it was too late. Mrs. Dockerty would demand to speak to his mother immediately.

But it wasn't Mrs. Dockerty on the phone. It was only Grandma.

A close call.

He sat back down on the floor and tried not to panic. No matter what, he vowed, when she got off the phone, he'd tell her.

But then there was a knock at the door and Tiny started to bark. So Mrs. Dockerty had decided to deliver the news face to face! This was worse! Grady leaped to his feet again. "I'll get it, Mom."

But it was only Laurel.

He looked down at her through the screen. "What do you want?" he asked, irritated with her for giving him such a scare.

"Mail for you!" She waved a taped-up piece of paper in front of him.

"Hello, Grady." The voice behind Laurel, coming from out on the porch, belonged unmistakably to Mrs. Dockerty. So there she was. The executioner of hopes and dreams and trips to California. She certainly hadn't wasted much time.

"Hi, Mrs. Dockerty." He opened the screen door and let them in, because what else was he supposed to do?

Tiny gave Laurel a lick on the face, and she began to wail.

"He won't hurt you, dear," said Mrs. Dockerty.

"That's right," said Grady. "Tiny's a real *good* dog."

When Mrs. Dockerty said, "How are you tonight, Grady?" he did not look at her eyes. He focused instead on her left ear.

"Oh, fine," he answered, watching the gold circle of her earring.

She asked him how practice had gone.

"Oh, fine."

Then she thanked him for taking Burgess to the Dairy Queen. Man. She was sneakier than Wendy-Alice, pretending like nothing was wrong.

Laurel peeked around her mother and waved the paper again.

"Laurie dear," said Mrs. Dockerty. "Didn't you promise Burgess you'd deliver that to Grady right away?"

Laurel smiled coyly. Then, when her mother was petting Tiny, she stuck out her tongue.

Grady took the note from her hand and said thanks, because he figured Mrs. Dockerty was probably listening, even if she wasn't watching. He shoved the paper into his pocket. What could Burgess possibly want now?

"Big secret, eh?" Mrs. Dockerty smiled approvingly at Grady. She didn't seem the least bit concerned that he was about to run away. But of course, she was just pretending until his mother hung up the phone. If only there was some way he could get them to go home!

"My mom likes the telephone a lot, Mrs. Dockerty," he said. "Sometimes she talks for hours. Maybe you should come back later."

Grady's mother hung up then and came out to say hello. Grady held his breath and waited for the bomb to drop.

But Mrs. Dockerty was even sneakier than he'd thought. She didn't say a word about his running away. Or about him yelling at her son. Instead she invited them for dinner. Maybe she was going to wait and announce it at the table! Boy, was *that* mean.

"Six o'clock all right with you?" she asked Grady's mother.

Grady's mother said six o'clock would be perfect and how nice of them to offer and could she please bring something.

"Oh, and Burgess had a note for Grady," Mrs. Dockerty added, smiling again.

Grady's mother raised her eyebrows. "Well," she said, smiling too. "How nice."

While the mothers discussed coleslaw and buns, Laurel squinted her eyes at Grady and stuck out her tongue again. Only farther this time. Grady gnarled his left hand and twisted his face into probably the best Grinch imitation he'd done since Halloween. She retreated instantly, with a whimper, behind her mother's skirt and stayed there until Mrs. Dockerty said good night.

After she'd closed the door, Grady's mother gave him a hug. "See how things work out when you give them a chance?" Her eyes were twinkling again. "I'll deal the cards. Grab us some cookies, will you?"

Grady nodded. Dinner with the Dockertys. An evening with Burgess. He didn't even want to imagine it.

He went into the kitchen and pulled the note out of his pocket. He peeled back the tape, and saw that Burgess had drawn a happy face on the bottom of the paper. Good grief. What was there for the kid to smile about?

He unfolded it. It read:

Dear Grady,
  Good luck doing you know what. If you need my help, I will. Don't worry, I won't say anything.

                                    Sincerely,
                                    Burgess Dockerty
P.S. I still like you.

How could Burgess still like him? The guy was amazing. He belonged in *Ripley's Believe It or Not*, under "Kid Who Never Gave Up."

And should he, Grady, believe it or not? Should he go back into the living room and tell his mother right then, or should he take a chance on the kid?

Grady thought about Burgess the motor-mouth. And Burgess the pest. And Burgess "Your Man on the Street." And it occurred to him that one thing the kid hadn't done through it all was lie. Maybe he really hadn't told his mother.

Grady looked again at the happy face. There were dots all over its nose that looked like warts. Grady guessed they were supposed to be freckles. Underneath it Burgess had written "Me."

Grady tapped his fingers against the cookie jar. Maybe he ought to trust the kid. At least for tonight. Until he had the chance to ask him a few questions. Like why was he doing this? Why, when he blabbed on anybody he could find in Iowa, was he going to keep his mouth shut this time?

Grady shredded the note and dropped it in the garbage can. He took three oatmeal cookies out of the jar, pulled a Yum-yum out of the treat box for Tiny, and headed back to the living room.

Yes, sir. He was out on a limb, all right. And it was getting skinnier by the minute.

10

The Odd Shop

The next morning, after Grady finished his paper route, he rang the Dockertys' doorbell. His stomach rumbled for breakfast, but it would have to wait another few minutes. Because before he did anything else, he needed to have a chat with Burgess.

It had taken him most of the night to figure out why the kid was going to keep his mouth shut about California. It was going to be blackmail. The kid wanted something. But what?

When Mrs. Dockerty opened the door, she whispered, "Burgess is still sleeping, Grady. Will you please come back later?"

So he did, twice. Once after he ate his cereal, and again after his trip to the bank on Kyle Baker's bike.

The last time he rang the bell, it was Dewey who opened the door.

"Hi, Grady," he said in between bites of drippy egg sandwich. "Burgess went someplace to do something, but I don't remember what."

Grady stomped back to his side of the house. He grabbed an apple from the refrigerator and bit into it with a noisy crunch. Burgess was doing this on purpose, not being around. And Grady knew why. He was getting even. Paying Grady back for calling him a pest. At this very moment he was probably laughing. Expecting Grady to be all worried trying to figure out what he was up to. Well, it was working.

Grady took several more loud bites of the apple, then pitched the core into the kitchen garbage. Why wait around until the kid decided to show up?

He snatched the dog leash off the hook in the back hall and called for Tiny. Then the two of them set out in search of the kid Grady hadn't been able to get rid of for the past two days. It was almost funny.

They walked down to the ball field. Burgess was nowhere around. They checked out the Dairy Queen, but he wasn't there, either. Grady clipped the leash onto Tiny's collar and headed for Rigotto's. He peeked in the front window. Nick was busy setting tables for the lunch rush, and the place was almost empty. Nick saw him and waved. Grady waved back and then walked

Tiny across the street to the gas station to ask Neal if he'd seen a skinny kid with red hair and glasses go by.

"About your age?" Neal asked. He was working under the raised hood of Mrs. Quade's Plymouth, examining the fan belt.

"Yeah."

"Red hair?"

"Yeah."

"And did you say skinny?" Neal wiped his hands on the rag that hung out of his pocket.

"Yeah."

"With glasses?"

"Yeah. He's the one."

"No, Grady, I ain't seen him. Been pretty busy."

The horn honked then, and both Grady and Tiny jumped. Mrs. Quade stuck her head out of the car window.

"Neeeal!"

Neal leaned around the hood of the car and hollered. *"Okay, Mrs. Quade! I'm done!"*

Somebody oughta make her turn up the hearing aids, thought Grady. He said thanks anyway to Neal and walked down the street toward Carlson's Odd Shop on the slim chance that Burgess had found the best store in town all by himself.

He tied Tiny to the bike rack out front and pushed open the heavy door. As usual, the Odd Shop smelled like floor wax and mothballs and Mrs. Carlson's perfume. He blinked, letting his eyes adjust to the dimness and the cluttered shelves.

He found Burgess standing in the third aisle, squeeze-testing the bulb of a squirting flower.

"Hey, Burgess," he said. "I've been looking all over for you."

"Really? I'm right here."

"I can see that. I want to talk to you."

"Sure thing," Burgess answered absently. Grady watched him pick up a pack of garlic gum from the shelf and hold it up to his nose. "It doesn't smell much."

"Of course it doesn't smell much. If it did, nobody would bite into it."

"Oh, I get it. But does it taste bad?"

"It tastes gross. I need to talk to you."

"Okay. But look at these, first." Burgess lifted a package of Peekaboo Peepers off its display hook. He read to Grady from the label. " 'Horrible, naked eyeballs,' it says. And look." He pointed to a drawing at the bottom of the orange package. "They float. Just think what a guy could do with these!"

As Burgess pressed his fingers against the cellophane package, Grady stood listening to the whir of Mrs. Carlson's ceiling fan. He was getting irritated. Here he'd come all this way and used up all this time, and the kid was hardly paying any attention to him. In fact, he was acting as if floating eyeballs were the only thing on his mind!

"Are you going to buy something, Burgess? Or just touch everything?"

Burgess didn't answer. He was staring up at the masks that hung above the shelves. He smiled dreamily. "If I had one of those, I could make a monster movie."

"They're hard to breathe in. How'd you like to be in the middle of a scene and pass out?"

"I wouldn't pass out. I'd stick straws up my nose. I could breathe real easy."

Yuck.

"Plus they're expensive, Burgess. I thought you were saving for a video camera."

"I gotta have one of these, Grady, no matter how much it costs." Burgess's voice was wistful and faraway.

So that was it! The kid wanted money!

Grady stuffed his fists into his pockets and looked up at the snarling face of Dracula, his fangs poised for the next meal. Maybe Burgess wouldn't demand the actual cash. Now that he'd seen the masks, maybe he'd expect Grady to buy him one. Well, he wouldn't. He couldn't!

"Burgess, are you almost done?"

"Sure thing, Grady. I guess I'll get the gum."

He picked up the pack of garlic gum and then began to drift slowly down the aisle until he saw the rubber hamburgers, and stopped. "I'm gonna get one of these, too. We can use it at dinner tonight."

Grady pointed in the direction of the cash register and said, "Come on."

It took a while for Burgess to pay Mrs. Carlson, because he kept asking her questions. How did invisible ink work? What kind of batteries went into the plastic hand? Would it crawl over carpet?

When they finally got outside, Burgess explained that he had to wait there for his mother. She was grocery shopping.

Well, okay. It didn't really matter *where* they had their little talk, did it? Grady untied Tiny's leash from the bike rack and leaned against the front window of the store, half sitting on the brick ledge. Above him, the Odd Shop's awning flapped in the breeze.

Burgess sat next to him and put the paper bag, with the gum and the hamburger inside, on his lap.

"So what'd ya want to talk about, Grady? You need my help?"

"Help?" Geez. The kid was unreal. "No, I don't need your help. I want to know what you want."

Burgess looked puzzled. "Huh?"

"Come off it, Burgess. *What do you want?* A mask? My baseball cards? Or are you holding out for money? If you are, you can forget it. I won't do it."

Now Burgess looked completely baffled. He leaned close, pushed his glasses up on his nose, and examined Grady like he was something under a microscope. "What exactly are you talking about?"

It was a real Academy Award performance.

"You just want to hear me say it, don't you? Okay, I will. What do you want in return for not telling anybody about me going to California?"

Burgess sat up in surprise. "Want something? I don't want something. Where'd you get a stupid idea like that?"

Grady was suddenly embarrassed. He didn't like the way Burgess said "stupid." *Stooopid*. It sounded like he thought Grady was some sort of idiot.

"Then why are you keeping the secret?"

"Because we made a deal. Don't you remember?"

"Of course I remember. But I didn't think you would."

"Why not?"

This was not going right at all. Burgess was supposed to be the one answering the questions.

"I guess I figured that when you figured I was running away, which I'm not, you'd figure the deal was off. Because running away would be a secret too big to keep."

Burgess stared at him. "You figured wrong, Grady," he said. "I don't break deals."

Grady looked away. "Then what about that Bunky kid in Iowa? The one who put sugar in his dad's gas tank? And what about Ralph and everybody else you wrote about in your paper? How come you decided to tell on them but not on me?"

"I didn't make deals with them. Most of them didn't even know me before I did the paper."

Grady ran his fingers over the smooth leather of Tiny's leash. He wasn't finished with the kid yet. "Plus I yelled at you. I called you a pest. I figured you were going to pay me back for that."

Burgess gave a small laugh. Like a guy does when something isn't funny at all. "No," he said. "That's happened lots of times."

"Oh."

"Dewey says if I want people to like me, I can't bug 'em all the time."

"Then why do you do it?"

Burgess began to fidget with the paper bag. He twisted the open end, untwisted it, and then twisted it up again before he finally answered. "Because if I don't bug people, they don't ever notice me."

"Oh."

Grady glanced over at Burgess, who was staring down at the crumpled bag in his lap. Now his feet were fidgeting. Man. He looked just like one of those kids in the orphan commercials on TV. Those kids Grady didn't like to see because he couldn't help them.

Grady wriggled on the ledge. Maybe Burgess really wasn't so bad. He was a terrible pest, for sure. But maybe he could be cured.

So what Burgess needed, then, was somebody around to help him. Somebody to show him how to act normal. He'd help the kid himself, if he wasn't so busy right now. If he wasn't moving to California in only a week. Maybe Kyle or Ian or Nick Rigotto could do it. Or Arthur Finley. He, Grady, just didn't have time to worry about the kid. So he stood up.

Burgess stood up too. "So when are you leaving for California?"

Grady stretched his arms. It felt good to be able to talk about it, even if it was with Burgess. "Soon as I hear from Mouse. And just for the record, I'm not running away. I wouldn't do that to my mom. I'm moving. My mom's gonna come out later. After she has time to think about it."

Burgess rolled up the bag and tried to stuff it in his front pocket, but the bag was too big. "How are you gonna get there?"

"We're taking the bus."

"Who's we?"

"Me and Tiny."

"You and Tiny? Together on the bus?"

Grady nodded.

"Oh, man," said Burgess, trying to squeeze the bag into one of his back pockets. "That's not going to work at all."

"Yes, it will."

"No, it won't." Burgess gave up on the pockets and tossed the bag into the air. "Wanna know why?"

Grady wished he hadn't let himself get into this. The kid was back to his old pushy self.

"So don't you want to know?"

Grady shrugged.

"I'll tell you why. Animals can't ride on the bus. It's a rule. My mom checked. She wanted to send our cats on the bus from Walding so I wouldn't sneeze in the car. But they said no pets."

Grady swallowed hard. Burgess was all wrong about this. He had to be. He thought of the dog his grandmother had seen on her bus. That proved it, didn't it? Probably it was just animals from Iowa that couldn't ride. Or maybe it was just cats. Sure, that had to be it. Cats, he knew firsthand, could be a real problem.

The Dockertys' rusted station wagon shimmied up to the curb then, with the front bumper dented and the engine ticking like a very large clock. When Mrs. Dockerty offered Grady and Tiny a ride home, Grady said yes because, just to be on the safe side, he was going to go home and call Audrey at the bus station right away. Even though Burgess was wrong about this.

They climbed into the car with the groceries and library books and with Laurel screaming to get out of her car seat. Mrs. Dockerty stepped on the gas, and Grady watched out the back window as they pulled away from the curb, leaving the Odd Shop behind in a cloud of blue exhaust.

11

Three, Two, One, Blast-off!

The news from Greyhound was worse than bad. Grady ran his fingers along the stripes on the kitchen wallpaper as he listened to the lady on the phone tell him first that Audrey was busy on another line and couldn't talk to him. Then he listened to her answer his question about Tiny riding the bus.

"Absolutely no pets, sir."

He explained about the dog on his grandmother's bus.

"It must have been a seeing-eye dog," she answered smartly. "They are the exception."

No pets on the bus? *No Tiny on the bus?*

"If dogs can't ride, then why do you have pictures of them on all of your buses?" Grady wanted to know. "It's not fair."

"Fair or not, sir, it's Greyhound policy."

And that wasn't all. It turned out that Greyhound had another policy the lady thought Grady should know.

"Let me remind you, sir, that persons under the age of twelve are not allowed to take a bus trip longer than five hours without an adult."

"*What?*"

She repeated the message, then asked, "Was there anything else?"

"No."

Numbly Grady set the telephone receiver back in its cradle. He sunk down into a kitchen chair. Tiny, who always seemed to know when something was wrong, looked up and lifted one paw. Grady held it in his hand and stroked the soft gold fur.

"Bad news, Tine," he whispered. "Worse than bad."

Why hadn't Audrey told him any of these things? Why had she let him think it was all going to work? He tried to remember just what Audrey had said. Oh, yes. She'd asked him if he was thinking of traveling alone, and he'd said no. He'd just forgotten to mention one small thing. That he was planning to travel with a dog.

He gave Tiny a pat and got up. He went to the sink, turned on the faucet, and splashed cold water on his face because it felt hot and puffy. Superman, he saw, was now standing on the windowsill. He'd forgotten to put him back in the coffee can.

He dried his face on the dish towel and picked up the plastic hero. "Jerk," he grumbled, and then he threw him at the garbage can. Superman hit the inside edge with a *thwap*. So much for good luck.

He climbed the stairs to his room, Tiny trotting up behind him, and collapsed across his bed. His quilt was a crumpled bundle on the floor. He pulled it up and stuffed it under his head.

The smartest brainstorm ever. What a joke. "Hunstiger," he whispered. "You are *stooopid*."

◎　◎　◎

He was still in his room, on his bed, staring at the spidery cracks in the ceiling, when his mother slammed the back door and hollered, "Grady! I'm home!"

Because he didn't answer, it took her a few minutes to find him.

"What in the world are you doing in bed? Are you sick?" She stood in the doorway, and Grady turned his head to look at her.

"I think so," he said. And it was pretty much true. He had a bad case of stupiditis.

His mother walked toward him in her stocking feet, and he listened to the crisp rustle of her uniform. She sat down on the edge of the bed. Gently she placed her hand on his forehead.

"You do feel warm, dear. When did this start?"

About the time I dialed the bus station, thought Grady.

"I don't know," he answered.

"I'll cancel our dinner with the Dockertys."

"No, Mom. You go. If I feel worse, I'll pound on the wall."

She slipped her fingers through Grady's hair. "I'll see." Then she stood up and reached into her pocket. "This came in the mail today. It's from the Stotts."

It was a postcard. With a picture of the ocean on it, and a long, white beach.

"I'll leave it here. You can read it when you feel better."

Grady watched her set the postcard on his desk. It couldn't be his invitation from Mouse yet. It was too soon. Well, whatever it said, it wouldn't matter anyway. Maybe he wouldn't even read it.

His mother bent down and gave him a kiss on the cheek. "Burgess will be disappointed," she said.

"He'll get over it."

She coaxed Tiny downstairs to feed him and let him out. And after stopping in Grady's room two more times to check on him, she finally went to the Dockertys'.

Through his open window, Grady listened to her cross the front porch and knock on the Dockertys' door. He heard tumbles and thumps on the other side of his wall, and then their door slammed and the porch was quiet.

The postcard was lying on top of the desk next to his radio. Maybe he should read it. What if the Stotts hated California and wanted to come home? He got up and went to the desk.

It said:

> Hi, Gwen and Grady!
> Arrived safely. Trip great. House terrific. Will call soon.
> Wish you were here. Love, Kathy, Matt & Mouse.

Oh, well.

He dropped the postcard on the floor and tried not to think about the ocean. He tried not to imagine playing Frisbee on that long, white beach ... with Tiny leaping and Mouse trying to outrun him. Most of all, he tried not to think about the terrific house, which probably had palm trees in the front yard and enough room for two guys to play catch underneath them.

It was hard work, all that trying. It made his head hurt. Maybe he should lie down again.

He was stuffing the quilt back under his head when he heard his front door open.

Was his mother back so soon?

No. It was Burgess. He walked into Grady's room holding a dinner plate and a can of 7-Up. "You sick?"

Grady turned his face to the wall. "I'm contagious. You better go home."

"That's not what your mom said."

"What does she know?"

"I thought she was a nurse."

"So?" Grady felt Burgess sit down on the end of the bed. He heard him bite into a chip.

"You sure seemed"—*crunch*—"okay this afternoon."

"Yeah well, it came on pretty fast." Didn't the kid know enough to leave a sick person alone?

"By the way, I asked my mom about animals on the bus, and I was right." Burgess bit through another chip.

"I know."

"What are you gonna do now?"

Grady rolled over and looked at Burgess. "Nothing. For the rest of my life."

Burgess took a bite of his hamburger. Grady watched the ketchup ooze out from under the bun and splat onto the sheet. Now his mother would think he was really sick. Bleeding and everything. It should be good for another whole day in bed.

"But, Grady, you can still go. I could take care of Tiny during the day, until your mom leaves for California. I'm not allergic to dogs, you know."

Grady shook his head. "Thanks, but there's this other rule too. It says that a person under twelve can't ride by himself on a long trip."

"How long?"

"I don't remember. Four or five hours."

Burgess picked up the pickle on his plate and swished

it around in his ketchup. Then he popped it in his mouth.

"Geez, Burgess."

"What?"

"Ketchup on the pickle. I'm sick, remember?"

"Oh. Sorry," he said, munching. "But, Grady. I still think you could make the trip."

"How? Grow wings and fly?"

"I'm serious. You don't have to take one long trip. Do a bunch of short trips instead."

"Huh?"

"Like this." Burgess set his plate on the floor and adjusted himself on the corner of the bed. "Make your first trip just to Minneapolis. That's not far. Then, when you get there, buy a ticket just to the next town. Do short trips like that and keep going toward California."

"But what if I got to Minneapolis and missed the bus to the next town?"

Burgess waved off his question. "Don't worry about that," he said confidently. "Buses do lots of short trips every day. They probably leave like every fifteen minutes. I know, because Dewey used to ride the bus to visit his girlfriend in Moline."

At first the whole thing sounded nuts. And impossible. But the more Grady thought about it, and the ocean, and Disneyland, and Mouse . . .

He sat up. He could do it. But what about Tiny? How could he leave the world's best dog behind? He tapped his fingers on his knees. Of course, they wouldn't be apart all that long, would they? No. Because his mother would be on her way to California in no time, and Tiny could ride with her. Keep her from getting lonesome. He might even like the car better than the bus.

Burgess was rocking on the end of the bed. "What d'ya think?"

"You'd take good care of Tiny when my mom's at work?"

"Sure thing."

"And feed him?"

"You bet."

"And play with him?"

"All the time."

"And talk to him a lot?"

"Of course."

"You'd have to keep him away from the cats."

"No problem."

"Say, Burgess, could I have a couple of those potato chips?"

Burgess handed him the plate. "Need any other help, Grady?"

Well, there was the paper route.

Burgess said it sounded like fun.

And the note to Coach Finley.

"You write it," said Burgess, "and I'll deliver it."

Burgess got up and wandered around the room while Grady tried to think if there was anything else. He watched Burgess look at his World Series posters, and his model cars, and his rock collection.

There was something else. One small something. Grady swung his legs over the edge of the bed and stood up. "Burgess," he said.

"What?"

"You want to be friends with me, right?"

"Right."

"So you'd like it better if I stayed here, right?"

"Right."

"Then why are you helping me leave?"

Burgess picked up a small agate and rolled it in his hand. He walked to Grady's bedroom window and looked out toward the big elm. "Because Dewey says it's not smart to hang on when it's time to let go."

Grady winced. Burgess sounded like a grown-up all of a sudden, and it made him wish he'd never asked the question. What did he care why Burgess did things, anyway?

He slumped back down on the bed and moaned. "I think I'm feeling sick again, Burgess."

"Gee, maybe it was the potato chips."

"Maybe."

After a couple long minutes, Burgess finally got the message and said, "See you tomorrow."

Grady listened to him bounce down the stairs and go out the front door. He smiled up at the ceiling cracks. The truth was, he'd never felt better in his life. Just look how things work out when you let them!

He reached down and picked up the postcard. He looked again at the ocean and the beach and the words on the back: *"Wish you were here."*

For sure the Stotts wouldn't write that unless they'd meant it. They wished he was there. They wished his mother was there too. And Tiny, even though they hadn't said so. They wanted things to be the way they used to be, just like he did, with all of them together and happy.

Grady leaned back against the quilt. Why was he wasting time waiting for Mouse's letter? Obviously they all wanted him to come to California. What other invitation did he need?

He jumped up and began to pace the room. There wasn't much he had to do, really. Pack. Write his mother. Write Coach Finley. His grandma he could write from California. Which left only showing Burgess the paper route. He could do it all in one morning, easy.

He set the postcard back on his desk and realized that he was hungry. Enormously hungry.

He walked out of his room toward the staircase, hooked his legs around the banister, and gave himself a push down. He would go tomorrow. Tomorrow it would be three, two, one, *blast-off!*

12

The Pioneer

Grady swung his duffle bag onto the kitchen table. He laid his backpack on the counter and checked through it one more time. He wanted to make sure his baseball cards weren't squishing the oatmeal cookies and the grapes that he'd packed. He stuffed Superman, whom he'd rescued from the garbage, in next to his ticket money, and then he zipped it closed. He was just about ready to go.

He pinned the letter he'd written to his mother onto the bulletin board by the phone. Then he stood back to take a look at it.

It was a good letter. No, it was a great letter. It mapped out his plans. It explained his reasons. The words "brave and resourceful" were underlined twice—

in the part about his being a pioneer. At the bottom of the page was a long row of *X*s and *O*s, which his mother would know meant hugs and kisses. And the letter was neat, besides. If Miss Lilyman saw it, she'd give him an A.

He smoothed out the crease in the center of the paper and smiled. For someone who didn't believe in writing letters, well, he was impressed.

The digital clock on the stove said 9:45 A.M. He was right on schedule. According to the plan he and Burgess had made earlier, Burgess would take over his duties with Tiny at ten o'clock. So there was plenty of time to explain things to the world's best dog. Where was Tiny anyway?

Grady called to him, and almost immediately he heard the retriever pad through the living room. He appeared in the kitchen doorway and yawned.

Grady squatted down in the middle of the floor. "Hey, Tiny," he said, trying to keep his voice peppy. "We need to talk."

Tiny ambled into the kitchen and sat himself down in front of Grady, his tail sweeping the floor. He gave Grady's face a lick.

"Tiny, I want you to listen to me."

Tiny gave him another lick.

"I mean it, Tiny. This is important. I'm leaving and—"

"Grady! Here I am."

It was Burgess. Grady turned and saw him cup his hands against the screen of the back door and peer in. He was early.

"You ready?"

Grady wrapped his arms around Tiny. "I love you, big guy," he whispered. "Just remember that." Then he stood up. "Yeah, Burgess, I'm ready."

Burgess opened the back door and walked in.

Grady hefted the backpack onto his shoulders. "Give Tiny one of his treats after I leave."

"Where are they again?"

"I told you before. They're under the sink. And don't let him out right away or he'll follow me."

Grady grabbed the nylon handles of his duffle and slid it off the table. He turned toward the back door, but Burgess stepped in front of him.

"This is for you, Grady." Burgess handed him a folded-up dollar bill.

Grady unfolded it. Only it wasn't a one-dollar bill. It was a five. The kid never knew when to quit. "Burgess," he said.

"What?"

"I thought you were saving for a video camera. Or one of the masks at the Odd Shop."

"I am. But I wanted to give you something. It's good luck from me. And thanks for getting me on the team."

Oh, man.

Grady looked down at the wrinkly bill in his hand.

No way could he take the kid's money. Not after, well, after everything. He set it on the counter. "You better keep it. I probably won't ever see you again, to pay you back."

"But it's a present."

"I can't take it, Burgess."

"Yes, you can."

Crimeny. There sure were a lot of different ways a person could be pushy. But it wasn't going to work. Because he wasn't going to take Burgess's money and then feel guilty the whole way to California.

"I've got plenty of money. But thanks anyway," he said, and he walked around Burgess to the door.

Tiny followed as if they were going off together like always, but Grady swallowed hard and said, "No, Tiny." He touched the tip of the retriever's black nose with his finger, and then he grabbed the door handle.

"So long, Burgess," he said. Then he pushed open the door and walked out.

◉ ◉ ◉

The Greyhound bus station was farther away from home than Grady remembered. But then he'd never walked to it before.

He passed by his school, the high school, and then the football and baseball fields in between. He passed the bowling alley, the Y.M.C.A., and the west side shopping center. In the distance he could see the top floors of the hospital, where his mother was working.

"Bye, Mom," he said. The words sounded funny. But then he'd never really had to say good-bye to his mother before. He hoped she wouldn't get too lonesome.

By the time he finally got to the station and pulled open the glass front door with the sticker on it that said DISCOVER AMERICA—GO GREYHOUND, his legs were aching. The straps of his backpack cut into his shoulders. He'd feel better if he could find a drinking fountain. If he could just sit down for a minute.

But the station was bustling, and there wasn't an empty seat in sight. A bus arrived from somewhere, and each time the glass door opened, a wave of bus fumes rolled past him. Passengers poured in carrying suitcases, talking, banging at the vending machines. Grady half expected to see his grandma come through the doors with her flowered case and a shoe box full of cookies for him under her arm.

It felt strange to be alone in the middle of so many people who seemed to know each other. But what had he expected? He was on his own this time. About to Go Greyhound and Discover America. He wasn't some little kid who was afraid to be by himself, was he? Of course not. Besides, he did know somebody. Audrey. She'd be glad to see him. If he could just drink some water and sit down first.

Bumped and jostled, he weaved his way around people and suitcases, looking for a drinking fountain. There wasn't one. He looked for an empty chair. There wasn't one of those, either.

He settled for a corner near the vending machines. Expensive vending machines that sold pop and sandwiches for a lot more than he paid at Rigotto's. Maybe he should have taken Burgess's money after all.

He set his duffle and backpack on the floor and leaned against the cool cement wall.

Across the room, above the ticket counter, was a large board with the bus schedule on it. It was a mess of numbers and letters that ran up and down and sideways. There must be some sort of trick to reading it. He'd ask Audrey. Because according to the plan, there were going to be lots of bus schedules between Johnson Falls and California.

He sat down on the floor and pulled off his left shoe. Three pebbles fell onto the gray tile. A girl with a tennis racket walked up to the vending machine next to him. She nearly stepped on his foot. He watched her push her coins into the slot and then listened to them jangle their way down through the machine. In a few seconds, a can of Diet Dr. Pepper rolled down through the tray. She grabbed it, popped the top, and walked away without ever looking up. She acted like he wasn't even there.

Grady fidgeted with his shoelace. Now that he

thought about it, nobody else had paid any attention to him either. No one had smiled at him or said "Hi" or even "Watch where you're going, kid" when he'd walked around trying to find a seat. What if he choked to death on one of his oatmeal cookies? Would anybody notice?

He shoved his foot back into his shoe. What he needed to do was just buy his ticket and forget about all these dumb people who didn't care if he lived or died. He lifted the backpack. It felt heavier than before. So did the duffle.

He stood at the end of the ticket line. On the wall behind the counter was a huge map of the United States. Bright blue lines, which he guessed were bus routes, crisscrossed the country. His eyes followed the longest line, which stretched way to the edge of the map. California. How long was it going to take to go that far? He wouldn't think about it, he decided, rubbing at the ache in his left leg. He just wouldn't think about it.

When he got to the front of the line, he set his backpack on the counter and said, "Hi, Audrey. It's me, Grady." It was going to be nice to see a smile.

The lady looked up from the papers she was stapling and frowned at him. She dabbed her forehead with a tissue.

"Audrey called in sick this morning," she said, annoyed. "And on such a busy day, for heaven's sake."

No Audrey? Grady's knees wobbled.

The lady went back to stapling papers. Without looking up, she told Grady she didn't have time to waste. Audrey shouldn't be visiting with friends at work anyway.

"But I came to buy a ticket."

She looked up and frowned again.

"To Minneapolis."

She set the stapler down and grumbled something Grady didn't quite catch. Something about not needing this today. She asked him for his age and his name.

"Look, Grady," she said, and she dabbed her forehead again. "The next bus to Minneapolis doesn't leave for two hours. I got a bunch of people on their way to Fargo, and I gotta get them settled first. You come back later. I'll help you then."

A wave of surprise washed through Grady's stomach.

"Don't buses go to Minneapolis every fifteen minutes?" he asked.

She shook her head and went back to her papers.

Two hours? What was he going to do for *two hours*?

He could eat lunch. Sure, that's what he could do. He could go outside and eat.

Gingerly he hung the backpack over one sore shoulder and picked up his duffle. There was one small patch of grass outside, next to the sidewalk. With relief he sank down onto it. In front of him the bus marked FARGO sat silent in the parking lot.

He unzipped his pack and took out the bologna sandwich and the Hi-C drink box he was saving for dinner. He poked the straw through the top of the waxy container. It wasn't smart, he knew, using up his supplies so early in the trip. But what else was there to do for two hours?

He took a long sip of the orange drink and a bite of the flattened sandwich, and thought about Burgess. The kid had been wrong about the bus schedule. And he'd forgotten where Tiny's treats were kept. It was not a good sign.

He took another bite of sandwich. It was the center bite. The part with no crust, usually his favorite. But today it didn't taste like much of anything, so he put it back in the Baggie.

What if Burgess forgot where Tiny's food was? Or what if he forgot to fill up the waterdish? *Or what if the kid just plain forgot Tiny?*

He stuffed the sandwich back into the pack. Maybe he should call Burgess. Go over things with him again. It would cost him a quarter, but Tiny was worth it.

He reached into his left pocket for one of his quarters. Only his fingers didn't touch quarters in the cotton lining of the pocket. They touched paper.

Shoot.

It was the note for Coach Finley. He'd forgotten to

give it to Burgess, and Burgess hadn't remembered to ask. Coach (not to mention the team) would think he was a first-class jerk, leaving town without a word. Double shoot.

He looked over at the Fargo bus. A man in a blue uniform was starting to load the storage compartment. Grady watched him toss bags and boxes and suitcases into it like he was in some kind of race. Pretty soon, Grady realized, *his* duffle would get tossed like that. What would happen to the plastic model Corvette he'd packed?

It took him a few minutes to haul his stuff back into the station to use the phone. He got the Dockertys' number and dialed it. Laurel answered.

"Hi, Grady!" she screeched, and then she hung up.

Splurging on a second precious quarter, he dialed again.

"Laurel, it's me again. Don't hang up."

"Bye, Grady!" Click.

Now what?

He lugged everything back outside to the grass and sagged down. How could so many things go wrong so fast?

He looked at the parking lot. While he'd been in the station, the Fargo bus had come to life. The diesel engine rumbled, and he could see the air around it vibrate with heat and fumes. People were boarding.

Grady watched the silver door swing open and the girl with the tennis racket disappear behind it. Then the door closed and she was gone. Swallowed up. He kept watching, expecting to see her appear at one of the bus windows, but they were some kind of glass he couldn't see through. Like the eyes of a giant insect, they stared at him. He was almost sure he saw the bus grin.

Maybe it wasn't a bus at all. Maybe it was some creature camouflaged as a bus. An extraterrestrial slug that ate earthlings. Nobody would ever see that girl or her tennis racket again. And in less than two hours the bus to Minneapolis would do the same thing to him.

Grady wrapped his arms around his legs and hugged them tight. "Stop it," he mumbled to himself. "Pioneers think positive."

He rested his chin on his knees. What he needed was something to do. Something to take his mind off the Fargo bus. And the Minneapolis bus. And Burgess. And Tiny. And the people who made him feel like the invisible man. And the map with the long blue line.

He snapped off a blade of grass. He could always sort his baseball cards—again. But he didn't feel like it. He could eat some grapes. But he wasn't hungry. Or he could go for a walk. But then he'd have to haul his backpack and his duffle with him, and he was sick of his backpack and his duffle. If only he hadn't packed his rock collection!

He watched the man in the uniform close the luggage-compartment door and walk around to the front of the bus. "All set!" he hollered.

Grady heard the grinding of the gears, and then the Fargo bus began to move. It inched itself, slow and heavy, across the parking lot until it reached the curb. With another wrenching of the gears and a belch of black smoke, it rolled into the street and lumbered off in the direction of the interstate.

Grady stared at the empty parking lot. At a sign that had been hidden from view by the Fargo bus. It said HAVE A NICE DAY!

Ha.

His eyes stung from the sharp diesel fumes, and he blinked to keep the tears back. He supposed the lady at the counter would be ready to sell him his ticket now. He should go back into the station and buy it. He blinked down at the grass.

Get up, Hunstiger. Go buy your ticket. You're a pioneer, remember? Brave and resourceful. Pioneers don't sit around worrying about their dogs or their baseball coaches or maps with long blue lines. Go buy your ticket. This is only the beginning.

This time as the glass door swung closed behind him, Grady saw that the station was almost empty. The man in the uniform was mopping the floor in front of the vending machines, and the lady behind the counter was eating a sandwich. He'd wait to buy his ticket until she finished eating. There wasn't any big reason to hurry.

He shuffled toward a set of empty chairs near the windows. Behind them on the wall was a bulletin board he hadn't noticed before. It was overflowing with want ads and announcements. He set his duffle and his pack, which each now weighed a ton, on the center chair. Then he gazed over the different colored papers. *Car for sale. Baby-sitter needed. Free kittens to good homes.*

There were garage sales and rummage sales and yard sales. Somebody was selling a fishing boat, almost brand new. Grady let his eyes roam the board until he saw a large piece of white paper with a photograph on it. It was a picture of a boy in a baseball uniform, holding a puppy in his arms. The boy was smiling into the camera. Below the picture, the word MISSING was printed in black.

Missing?

Grady's stomach lurched. How could a kid from Johnson Falls be missing?

But the information written below didn't say how. It gave only the boy's name and birthday. Then the message: IF YOU SEE TOMMY, PLEASE CALL THIS NUMBER. The word "please" was underlined.

The kid must have gone someplace and gotten lost. That had to be it. He couldn't have been kidnapped. Not in Johnson Falls. And he certainly wouldn't have run away. He was smiling and he had a dog and he played baseball. Who'd be stupid enough to leave all that?

Grady looked at Tommy, and Tommy looked back until, for a split second, it wasn't Tommy. It was a picture of Grady Hunstiger, first baseman for the Rigotto Royals, taken two years ago with his tiny puppy.

Grady's throat felt thick. He tried to swallow, but he couldn't. Something inside his stomach was bouncing like a Mexican jumping bean. And his eyes were stinging again. He turned around and slid down into the chair next to his backpack, because if he kept standing, he knew he'd be sick.

What was he doing taking off on a trip halfway across the country? What was he doing leaving Tiny with Burgess? And the Royals without a first baseman? And his mother all alone?

He blinked down at the pink speckles in the tile. *How had he ever gotten himself into this?*

He unzipped his backpack, letting his fingers dig until they touched Superman. He pulled out the old toy and held it in his hand.

Mouse. He was doing this for Mouse. So they could be a team again. So they could live in a big white house and play catch under the palm trees in the yard and go to Disneyland and swim in the ocean.

Only it wasn't going to work.

Grady squeezed his eyes shut.

Things would never be the same. Ever again. His mother had been right.

Grady felt someone sit down beside him. He opened his eyes.

Coach Finley was looking at him, his badge bright gold against the dark of his uniform.

"Hey, Hunstiger," he said gently. "What's up?"

Grady wiped the wetness off his cheeks with the back of his hand. "Not much, Coach. What are you doing here?"

"Not much, Hunstiger. What are you doing here? You going someplace?"

Grady looked down at Superman. He slid the plastic hero back into his pack.

"Home. I'm going home."

"I'm mighty glad to hear that." Coach sounded relieved. As if he knew all about kids leaving home on Greyhound buses. "How about a lift?"

Grady nodded.

"Let me give you a hand," he said.

Grady watched him stand up and swing the duffle, and the backpack, over his shoulder.

"What in the world have you got in here, Hunstiger? Rocks?"

"Just a few."

Coach laughed.

Grady stood up, his knees a little shaky, and pointed to the picture of Tommy. "What happened to that boy, Coach?"

"Nobody knows, Grady," he answered. "Not yet, anyway."

Then he put his arm around Grady's shoulder.

"Ready, Hunstiger?"

"Ready, Coach."

"All right then. Wagons, ho!"

13

Blown to Bits

Coach Finley agreed to drop Grady off at the far end of Cooney Avenue, by the creek bridge, instead of driving the police car right up in front of the house. So the neighbors wouldn't think Grady'd been out robbing banks or something.

"Thanks, Coach," said Grady as he lifted his backpack and duffle off the front seat. "I'll walk right home. I promise."

Coach smiled. "I'm not worried, Hunstiger. We've got practice tonight. I expect you to be there."

"I will be." Grady slammed the car door.

Coach waved, then shifted the gears and drove off. He hadn't said much to Grady on the ride home except "If you ever need to talk . . ." Then he'd lent Grady his handkerchief and started in on batting averages of the

New York Yankees and the Minnesota Twins and the Rigotto Royals. Somehow, Grady had expected a lecture.

He stuffed Coach's handkerchief into his pocket and gazed up at the street. Everything looked the same, which, oddly, was a surprise. So very much had changed.

He hoisted the pack carefully over his sore shoulders and began his walk home.

He passed Mrs. Quade's. She was reading on her porch swing, the sprinkler in her yard doing its usual *cha-cha-cha* as it sprayed water over the grass. Farther down the block some little kids were splashing around in a wading pool. Next door to them Wendy-Alice's father was outside painting shutters.

They were all acting like nothing was wrong.

But his life had exploded. Hadn't they noticed? His smartest brainstorm ever—blown to bits. *Ka-booom!* Hadn't they heard it?

He pulled Coach's handkerchief out of his pocket and wiped his nose. His right arm was aching again, so he shifted his duffle to his other hand. Then he crossed to his side of the street.

The Cooney house loomed in front of him. He blinked up at it. The Dockertys' window shades were pulled against the afternoon sun, and it made the old place look sleepy.

"Hello, house," he whispered hoarsely. "I'm back."

But the house didn't wake. Maybe it didn't care that he was back again. Or even that he'd left.

Grady stepped off the sidewalk and ducked behind the pines in the side yard, dried needles crunching under his shoes. He needed to get ready for what was going to happen next. Burgess. The kid was going to fire questions at him a hundred miles an hour.

He closed his eyes and let one of the prickly boughs brush against his cheek. Maybe he'd tell Burgess the Minneapolis bus broke down. Or the Greyhound drivers went on strike. Or the tickets were all sold out. Or maybe he ought to just punch him one, finally. Like he should have done that first day, when the kid wouldn't mind his own business. Sure, that's what he'd do.

He opened his eyes and stepped out to the yard. He might as well get it over with. But he certainly didn't have to walk up the front steps like a one-man parade, so he went around to the back gate.

Any second now Tiny would come racing. Followed by Mister Motor-Mouth.

But the backyard was quiet. Grady swung open the gate. Probably once he reached the back door, Tiny would come flying, with Burgess right behind. Then the questions would start up.

He crossed the yard and climbed the porch steps. But Tiny didn't come flying. Grady gave the back-door handle a yank and walked in.

The kitchen was dim and shadowy. Except for the

low hum of the refrigerator, there wasn't a sound. Grady stood by the door and looked around the room.

The window was partway open, the curtains rippling noiselessly in the breeze, and everything was just as he'd left it: his cereal bowl and spoon in the dishrack, his empty juice glass in the sink. The Rice Krispies box was on the counter, the top flap open, and the chair he'd sat in for breakfast was still pulled out from the table. His kitchen. His things. But all of a sudden he felt like a stranger.

"Tiny?" he said, hesitating. "Tiny? I'm home."

Maybe the dog was upstairs.

"Tiny!"

Grady listened for the *pad-pad* of the dog's paws against the upstairs floor. But there was nothing.

He set his duffle and Coach's handkerchief on the counter and walked across the kitchen.

"Tiny!" He called again.

Nothing.

He eased his backpack off his shoulders and laid it on the desk by the phone. Now he was going to have to go next door and find Burgess so he could get Tiny back. Then he'd have to say hello to the whole Dockerty family.

He slumped against the door frame and tried to rub the kink out of his left shoulder. In front of him, still pinned to the bulletin board, was the letter to his mother. She was never going to see it. Nobody would.

And it had been the best one he'd ever written. Except for one thing.

It wasn't true.

He wasn't a pioneer and he wasn't brave and resourceful and he wasn't Grady the Great anymore. Mouse wasn't the Mighty Mouse either, but he probably already knew that. Just like Grady's own mother did. Everybody had known but him. Stoooopid ol' Hunstiger.

He unpinned the letter, tore it up, and let the pieces fall into the kitchen garbage. Then he headed over to the Dockertys'.

He rang their doorbell three times, but nobody seemed to be home there either. Just what was going on? In only a few hours he'd been deserted.

He was about to leave when Dewey peeked his head out their dining-room window. "Hi, Grady."

"Hi. Where's Burgess?" He sure never thought he'd say that again.

"At the ball field. Said something about pitching practice."

"Thanks."

◉ ◉ ◉

Grady stood on the corner of the boulevard and looked over at the field. He could see the two of them, Burgess and Tiny, horsing around with the baseball. Burgess was pitching, Tiny was catching, sort of. They were alone.

Grady felt his throat tighten up again. He took a steadying breath and crossed the street. He'd just stepped onto the grass when Tiny spotted him.

One bark, and the dog began to run. His ears back, his head low, his paws barely touching the ground, he bounded straight toward Grady. He streaked past Burgess on the pitchers' mound and flew past second base. A flash of russet gold.

Grady knelt down in the rough grass so the dog could knock him over.

And he did.

Flat.

"Hey, big guy," Grady whispered as he buried his face in the silky fur of Tiny's neck. "Hey."

By the time Tiny let Grady sit up, Burgess was bobbing across the infield toward them. In one hand was his glove, two baseballs, a lunch bag, and the end of Tiny's leash, which was bouncing along on the ground behind him. In the other hand he lugged Tiny's water pail.

And here Grady'd been afraid the kid would forget all about Tiny. It almost made him smile.

Burgess stopped once in midfield. He set the pail on the ground and wiped his forehead with the back of his hand. Then he picked up the pail again and came the rest of the way. Tufts of pumpkin hair were sticking out from the sides of his baseball cap. His new Royals jersey was covered with dust, and his glasses were crooked, of course. Water was sloshing every which way out of the pail.

He stood in front of Grady for a long time before he said, in a voice that sounded like it had all happened to him, "It blew up, didn't it? The whole plan."

Grady leaned his head against Tiny's shoulder. His eyes were stinging again, and he wished he still had Coach's handkerchief. "Yeah, Burgess," he answered. "It blew sky high."

Burgess put the pail down, and the glove, and the baseballs, and the leash. Then he sat down on the grass and opened the lunch bag. He pulled out a Yum-yum dog treat and gave it to Tiny. Then he stuck his hand back in the bag and took out a large, melty chocolate cookie and a can of grape drink. He split the cookie and said, "Here, Grady." Then he popped the top of the grape drink, took a swig, and handed it over.

They sat together, eating. Tiny lay between them, his head in Grady's lap. Nobody asked any questions. Nobody gave any answers. Nobody said anything at all, until the ants found them.

Tiny pushed one around with his nose and sneezed. Burgess started wriggling. Grady slapped at two of them on his knee and another one on his ankle. Then he stood up.

"Guess it's time to go home, Burgess."

"Yep."

14

The Bug

Grady tossed the fluorescent-orange tennis ball into the air and watched it spin toward the maple trees in the backyard. It landed with a *plop* in the hammock.

"Fetch, Tiny," he said, and Tiny bolted down the porch steps after it. Grady watched him pick it up with his teeth and then trot back across the yard. Tail waving, he climbed up the first two steps and deposited it, like a gift, in Grady's lap.

"You're the best, Tine. No doubt about it." Grady rubbed the retriever on the nose.

As he threw the ball again, Grady heard the Dockertys' screen door open behind him and Burgess bounce out. He could tell it was Burgess without even looking.

"Why do you do that, Burgess?" he asked.

"Do what?"

"Bounce."

Burgess sat down next to him on the step. "I don't know."

"Well, it looks dumb."

"Really?"

"Really."

Tiny loped up the sidewalk with the ball.

"Can I throw it, Grady?"

Grady shrugged, and Burgess pulled the ball from Tiny's mouth.

"This one's gonna be a homer, Tiny. So get ready!"

Burgess wound up and hurled the ball. It sailed almost to the top of the farthest maple, then landed in the corner of the yard. Tiny ran hard until he reached it, then stood pawing at the ground. He looked back and barked. The ball was wedged between the slats of the fence.

"Nice going, Burgess."

Burgess jumped up and speed-walked toward Tiny. Like he was trying to hurry without bouncing. It looked even dumber. Oh, well.

Grady leaned against the porch railing. He'd have plenty of time now, to show the kid how to act normal. Next, they'd have to do something about those messed-up glasses.

Grady watched Burgess get down on his hands and knees next to the fence and yank out the ball. Actually, he thought, the kid was coming along pretty well. Two days had passed since the big fiasco at the bus station, and Burgess still hadn't asked a question, which had been a surprise. The kid's curiosity had to be about burning a hole in him.

His mother, too, had surprised him. Although she knew nothing about the trip, because he'd thrown the letter away, she'd been acting strange. She'd even offered to help him buy a new bicycle. So he could get around and enjoy the summer, she'd said.

Burgess threw the ball toward the other end of the yard and then walked back up the steps. He sat down again, next to Grady.

"Trouble's comin'," he said.

"What?"

"Trouble. It's comin' down the alley."

"What are you talking about, Burgess?"

Burgess pointed past the maple. "Look for yourself."

It was Wendy-Alice and Elizabeth.

"Let's get out of here," said Grady. "I don't feel like fighting with her today."

But it was too late. The girls were almost at the back gate.

Tiny, Grady noticed, had disappeared around the side of the house. Smart dog.

"Hi yaaaaa, Grady," Wendy-Alice drawled. She leaned against the gatepost and shot Grady a metallic smile. "Aren't you going to invite us in?"

"No."

Grady watched her whisper to Elizabeth, and then both girls giggled. Geez, they were a pain.

Wendy-Alice opened the gate and Elizabeth followed her into the backyard. They sauntered up the sidewalk toward the back porch, their droopy earrings swinging.

"What d'ya want, Bossyface?" Grady asked.

"Matthew's address."

"I lost it."

"Ha. I'm going to stay here until I get it. So give it to me."

"But, Bossyface," said Grady innocently. "Mouse hates you. He used to tell me so every day. 'I hate Wendy-Alice,' he'd say in the morning. 'I hate Wendy-Alice,' he'd say at lunch. 'I hate Wendy-Alice,' he'd say before he went to bed. Can't you take a hint?"

Wendy-Alice squinted up her eyes until they looked like little bullets. "You're a creep, Hunstiger."

"So leave."

"Not till I get what I came for." Wendy-Alice toyed with one of her earrings. "You're just jealous because I like Matthew and not you."

That was a laugh.

She cupped her hand over Elizabeth's ear and whispered again. Elizabeth giggled again.

Grady wished he could think of something to do that would shut them up and make them go home. For good. But his great ideas never worked with Wendy-Alice. Plus, his great ideas hadn't been so great lately.

He reached into his front pocket and pulled out two strawberry candies. He handed one to Burgess. "Too bad I don't have enough to go around," he said loudly.

The girls ignored him.

Grady unwrapped the candy and popped it into his mouth, letting the tart, sweet juice coat his tongue. He poked Burgess with his elbow. "Eat it," he said, under his breath.

"But I don't like strawberry."

"Eat it anyway. And slurp it."

The two girls quit whispering, and Wendy-Alice took a step closer to the porch. She zeroed in on Burgess. "I don't see your seedy little cats. I bet they made you get rid of 'em, huh?"

Burgess didn't answer.

Grady bit noisily into the sugary center of the candy. "Why don't you two get back on your brooms and go home?"

Wendy-Alice flashed him a sly smile. "I'm not leaving until you give me what I want. If you're going to be stubborn, Bethie may have to bring our lunches over. Think about it, Hunstiger. We could have a picnic together right here in your crummy backyard. Wouldn't that be fun?"

"Yes!" answered Burgess, and before Grady could grab him, he'd hopped down the steps toward the girls.

And here Grady'd thought the kid was making progress. What a dope.

Grady watched him look up at Wendy-Alice, who was at least a foot taller.

"As you know," he was saying, "I just moved in. So I'm trying to meet everybody and make friends."

Wendy-Alice smirked. "Isn't that nice, Bethie? The little boy is trying to make friends."

On cue, Elizabeth smirked too.

Wendy-Alice's eyes narrowed. "Where'd you and your cats come from, little boy? Mars?"

Grady closed his eyes. He didn't want to watch this.

"No," Burgess answered politely. "We just arrived from Hong Kong."

Hong Kong? Grady popped his eyes open. What happened to Iowa?

Elizabeth stopped smirking.

"We move lots. So I have to make friends fast," Burgess continued. "You see, my father is a famous scientist. He invents things. Right now he's doing experiments for Channel Six TV."

Wendy-Alice stopped smirking.

"We're in Johnson Falls to test some of my father's inventions on people and make reports. For television. Then we're leaving for Australia."

Where in the world, Grady wondered, was the kid getting this stuff?

"Television?" asked Wendy-Alice.

"Yup," answered Burgess. "My father is looking for people to be in the experiments. Special people."

Wendy-Alice looked at Burgess with new interest. "Can you prove it?"

"Sure. Did you see the trailer we pulled behind our car the day we moved in?"

Both girls nodded.

"Did you see us unload it?"

"No."

"That's too bad. It was full of my father's experiments. You could have seen them."

Grady blinked in amazement. The kid had an answer for everything.

"What if we don't believe you?"

Burgess shrugged. "Doesn't matter to me. You probably couldn't be in the experiments anyway."

Wendy-Alice put her hands on her hips and glared down at Burgess. "Why not? What's the matter with us?"

Burgess put his hands on his hips and looked up at Wendy-Alice. "Not just anybody can be in them. Channel Six only wants important people. They have to be real intelligent and wise and stuff. You know, important."

"Well," said Wendy-Alice. "I've never been part of an experiment or anything, but I'm like that. Do the people get to be on television?"

It was a good thing, thought Grady, that he was sitting down. Because otherwise he would have fallen over. Wendy-Alice was going for it. And Burgess! The kid was unbelievable. Not once had he even cracked a smile. Grady put both his hands over his mouth because he knew *he* couldn't do that.

"Be on television? Absolutely." Burgess went on without a hitch. "It's a real honor to be part of these experiments. To the progress of America and everything."

"So why can't you give me a try? I'm the smartest person in the class. Right, Grady?" Wendy-Alice looked anxiously at Grady.

Without moving his hands away from his mouth, Grady nodded.

"What about me?" Elizabeth asked, pouting. "You two are acting like I'm not even here. I'm just as smart as Wendy-Alice."

Wendy-Alice scowled at her.

"Well, almost as smart."

Burgess hesitated. He tapped at the sidewalk with the toe of his shoe.

"Plus, I've already earned nine badges in Girl Scouts," Elizabeth pleaded.

"You have not," snapped Wendy-Alice. "You've only

got seven." Wendy-Alice turned to Burgess. "I have ten. And mine are already sewn on my uniform. I could wear it when I went on television."

Burgess continued to tap at the sidewalk.

"So how about us?" Wendy-Alice asked impatiently. "We'd be perfect. And you *do* want to be friends, don't you?"

Burgess looked up. "Oh, yes. Um, I guess it would be okay. I'll check my father's schedule and see what this week's experiment is."

He turned from the girls and climbed the steps. As he passed by, Grady peeked up at him. For an instant their eyes met, and Grady saw a smile spread across Burgess's face. A long, slow, lizardy smile that made Grady nearly burst. Quickly he looked away.

As the Dockertys' screen door slammed shut, Grady swallowed hard. He bit at the inside of his lip until it hurt. He had no idea what Burgess was planning, but whatever it was, he, Grady, was not going to goof it up.

"I bet they didn't ask *you* to do research, did they, Grady?" Wendy-Alice's voice was smug. "I bet they checked with the school and found out that Miss Lily-man gave you a D, and that was the end of that."

Without looking up, Grady nodded. He didn't trust himself even to speak.

When Burgess came back outside, he was carrying a video camera.

Where had *that* come from? But of course, Grady couldn't ask. Not now. It was the critical moment.

"Grady," Burgess said in a serious, businesslike, no-nonsense voice, "could you help us here?"

Grady, being extra careful not to make eye contact, stood up.

Burgess focused the camera and handed it to him. "Just stay here on the porch. Push this button to start it, and then push it again when we're finished."

Grady nodded. Then he hefted the camera onto his shoulder and looked through the viewfinder. He saw Burgess walk down the steps to the girls.

"Is this for television now?" Wendy-Alice sounded upset. "I wanted to wear my uniform."

"Oh, no," assured Burgess. "That comes later. This is just for my dad. Ready?"

"Ready," said the girls.

"Okay, Grady," said Burgess. "Push the button."

Grady did.

Burgess stood next to the girls and looked at the camera. "This week's experiment is top secret," he announced. "Highest priority."

"Wow!" said both girls, smiling into the camera.

Then Burgess reached into his back pocket and pulled out a rumpled paper bag.

Where, Grady tried to remember, had he seen that before?

Burgess opened the mouth of the bag.

"What is it?" Wendy-Alice asked, breathless.

Burgess cleared his throat and said, ceremoniously, "Gum."

"*Gum?*" Both girls echoed.

GUM! Grady leaned against the porch railing to steady himself. So that's where he'd seen the bag. It was Odd Shop gum. Garlic gum. Oh, brother, oh, brother, oh, brother!

"Yes," answered Burgess. "But it's not just any old gum. It's space gum. There's nothing else like it in the world. We're testing it for astronauts."

Grady took a big breath and tried to hold the camera straight. He watched Wendy-Alice's face sink.

"But I'm not supposed to chew gum," she whined. "Because of my braces. I get in trouble when I do."

Burgess waved his hand through the air, as if he were erasing an invisible chalkboard. "No problem. This gum doesn't stick to metal. A girl in Madrid who wore braces chewed a whole pack."

Relief washed over her face.

"How many sticks do we get?" Elizabeth asked hungrily.

"One a day for a week."

"Wow!"

Burgess stuck his hand in the bag and pulled out two sticks of gum.

"But you have to promise one thing," he said, shaking the gum in their faces with each word. "You have to keep a diary. So my father can study you. So Channel Six can see how you like it."

"Sure."

"Easy."

"Anything for America."

Grady took another breath. He pressed his legs together, because if Burgess didn't hurry up, he was going to wet his pants right there on the porch.

Burgess held out the two sticks of gum.

Carefully the girls took them. And unwrapped them. They smiled into the camera, and then they put the gum in their mouths.

Chomp.

Chomp.

Chomp.

"I can tell you one thing right off," said Elizabeth, her mouth in a funny shape. "It takes like garbage. I don't think the astronauts will like this."

"Really?" asked Burgess.

Elizabeth nodded.

"Gee, that's too bad." Burgess turned toward Wendy-Alice. "So what do YOU think?" he yelled. "Miss Bossyface pain in the neck?"

For a split second, Wendy-Alice looked dumbfounded. Then suddenly she understood, and her face lit up with fury.

"*Youuuuuuuuu!*" she wailed, and she kicked at Burgess, aiming for his shin.

But Burgess was fast. He jumped back, and then he began to laugh. At first it was only a "Hee-hee." Then a "Ha-ha." And when he couldn't hold it in anymore, he let loose.

Wendy-Alice began hopping up and down like a chicken, pulling at her mouth. Elizabeth tried to help her. But Wendy-Alice kept shoving her away.

Grady heard Tiny barking from somewhere, then a moment later he was on the scene too, bounding back and forth between Elizabeth and Wendy-Alice as if he were trying to join the fun.

The Dockertys' back door swung open behind him, and he felt a tap on his arm. It was Laurel.

"Don't bump me," he said.

Then he kneeled down and balanced the camera on the railing because he couldn't hold it steady another minute. This was one of the best things he'd ever seen. Better even than Indiana Jones. He certainly wasn't going to muck it up with a shaky tape!

Wendy-Alice opened her mouth and tried to scream something, but it was impossible to understand what. The rubbery gray goo had wound itself all through her braces, twisting around the metal bands, covering the wires.

But the more Wendy-Alice pulled, the more it wound. Like taffy on a hot sidewalk, it stretched and stretched and wouldn't let go. Strands of it, Grady saw, were stuck to her chin and one earring.

"Big icky!" exclaimed Laurel.

"*You—You—pissants!*" hollered Elizabeth.

"*Yaaaaah!*" cried Wendy-Alice.

Elizabeth stood over Burgess, who was now rolling around on the grass, nearly hysterical. "*We'll get you for this!*" she screamed. "*Gimme your name!*"

Grady pushed the camera button off. Then he walked down the steps. Calmly he went to Tiny and gave him a pat on the head. He gave Elizabeth a nice big smile and Wendy-Alice an even bigger one. And then he said, because he didn't want girls running all over Johnson Falls calling the kid *Burrr-gess*, "This is the Bug. He's dangerous. Leave him alone. Leave *us* alone. Or we *will* show this tape to Channel Six!"

All of a sudden Grady realized his head was loaded with great ideas. Tons of them.

"He runs a newspaper, too," he shouted. "Maybe he'll tell this story all over Minnesota. Maybe we'll send a news flash to Mouse . . ."

Grady began to laugh. Why, he could go on all day. But the girls, he saw, had slammed the back gate and were already racing down the alley, Tiny barking his good-bye.

Grady turned and looked at Burgess. The kid really did belong in *Ripley's*. Under "Surprise of the Century." And here Grady'd thought he needed help. Ha!

"Way to go, Bug," he said, and flopped down on the grass.

Burgess grinned.

"But where'd you get the camera?"

"My uncle. He bought a new one, so we got his used one. Wanna go inside and rewind the tape?"

Grady leaned back on his elbows and smiled. "Only if we can watch it a few hundred times."

15

Grady the Great

On the twentieth of June, the mailman climbed the steps of the old Cooney house and handed Grady a letter. It was from Mouse.

Grady took the stairs to his room three at a time, then flopped down on his bed and tore open the envelope. The letter read:

Yo, Grady the Great!

I am here, but it was a long ride. I threw up three times in the car.
How's Tiny?
California is neat, but I got here too late to sign up for baseball. I am not doing much.
I'll find the address of a movie star and you

*can give it to Bossyface. Tell her it's mine. Fake
out!*

What happened that was so horrible?

*I heard my parents talk about you and your
mom visiting us at the end of the summer. Your
mom has two weeks' vacation, but don't say
anything because it is a surprise for you, I think.
You better come!*

*Bring Tiny and lots of plastic bags to throw up
in.*

*I wish I was back pitching for the Royals. Tell
Nick to stay with the fastball.*

At the bottom of the letter Mouse had drawn a picture of the Hunstiger's Volkswagen, with the words
CALIFORNIA EXPRESS across its side. He'd drawn Grady's
mom standing next to the car waving and Tiny hanging out the back window. He'd drawn Grady slumped
over in the front seat of the car with his head in a bag.

Very funny.

Underneath the drawing he'd signed:

> *Your best friend,*
> *The Mighty Mouse*

Grady leaned back against his quilt and smiled up at
the spidery ceiling cracks. He'd been right after all.
Some things *don't* change.

What would happen, he wondered, when his mother

saw California? What would she think of the beach and Disneyland and being with the Stotts again? Maybe she'd want to move there.

He read the letter two more times before he folded it and slid it under his pillow. He'd just have to wait and see.

He went downstairs to the back hallway. He lifted the tied-together laces of his cleats off their hook and grabbed his mitt. He put his baseball cap on backward and then opened the screen door. Tiny was waiting for him on the porch.

"You ready, Tiny?"

The retriever danced in place.

"Good."

Grady stepped out and let the door slam behind him. It was time to grab the Bug and hustle over to the field, because the Royals had a lot of work to do. The exhibition game against the Angels (planned and organized by guess who) was less than two weeks away, and the girls had been handing out fliers all over Johnson Falls. Neal, at the gas station, even had one taped to the side of his premium pump.

One thing was for sure. The Rigotto Royals absolutely, positively, had to win.